War.

C0-BJL-815

'/22
'/2+

THE
OLD GUYS
BACK TO BAGHDAD

Mike Ryan

Don & Marion,
It has been fun re-writing this past year.
Best Wishes,
Mike Ryan

Ryan Enterprises

This book is a work of fiction. The background, names, characters, places and incidents are products of the author's imagination or are used fictitiously. Any resemblance to actual events, locations or persons living or dead is purely coincidental.

© Copyright 2007 Mike Ryan

All rights reserved. No part of this publication may be reproduced, stored in a retrieval system, or transmitted, in any form or by any means, electronic, mechanical, photocopying, recording or otherwise, without the written prior permission of the author.

ISBN: 978-1-4251-4274-2

Note for Librarians: A cataloguing record for this is available from Library and Archives Canada at www.collectionscanada.ca/amicus/index-e.html

Edited by Mike Sirota
Cover design and illustrations by Eric Chauvin

Manufactured and printed in the United States of America

Order this book online at www.trafford.com/07-1782
or email orders@trafford.com

Most Trafford titles are also available at major online book retailers.

10 9 8 7 6 5 4 3 2 1

Book Dedication

This book is dedicated to my wife Cherie
who supported me in this new endeavor
every step of the way. I love you.

&

The men and women who have risked
it all by living, working and fighting in Iraq
to support America's efforts to build
peace and freedom for its people.

Prologue

Vietnam – 1965

PRIVATE DAVE OWENS winced as the sharp pain of the bullet seared the flesh on his left shoulder, but he kept on crawling. Owens, nicknamed 'DO' for his initials and his ability to *do* almost anything asked of him, was exhausted. He had been awake for over twenty-four straight hours. The eight-man squad he'd been assigned to had been under fire since just before nightfall and he was tired of it. Even though he was new to the Army, fresh out of boot camp and experiencing his first firefight, he knew instinctively that somebody needed to do something to regain control of the battlefield, or it would be all over for them. They were too close to enemy lines…more North Vietnamese combatants would be on their way soon. This small group of soldiers out on a critical reconnaissance mission aiding the U.S. advisors couldn't hold out forever in a damned trench, and the rest of the platoon was too far away.

Their orders were to *not* engage the enemy. They were only there to collect information, which could be used by others. Now, however, they weren't being given a choice.

The non-com team leader had crawled out of the trench first. The machine gun, which had been quiet for a few minutes, poured bullets in the man's direction. He flew backwards several feet before landing hard. Owens, following close behind, quickly dove to the ground or he too would have been riddled with bullets. After it grew quiet again, he crawled to the downed man.

"Talk to me Johnson. How bad is it?"

"Bad enough." He coughed. "I'm hit in the chest. It…hurts. Oh man…it hurts so bad. I…can't breathe."

"Don't worry. I'll get you to cover."

Owens took a handful of the injured man's shirt at the collar and started slowly dragging him to safety. More bullets screamed overhead as the enemy machine gun spat out another blast. The wounded soldier cried out in pain.

"I know this makes you hurt even more, but it's better than staying out here. Hang on; I'll get you back."

Owens dug his heels into the dirt for leverage and started pulling. One foot, two, then three. Foot by foot he dragged the now limp body toward safety. With one last tug they finally reached the trench, where several outstretched hands helped finish the task. A medic quickly attempted to stabilize the injured man, while Owens, now covered with mud, lay on his back breathing heavily.

By mid-morning their circumstances hadn't improved. The bullets screamed overhead just often enough to be nerve-wracking to those in the hole. Just *holding the line* as ordered by the top brass was not enough for Owens. More was needed, and it was needed right now. He leaped from the protection of the trench and started crawling the hundred yards between himself and that damned machine gun, using the cover of ground fog, which would likely be lifting soon. It couldn't be *that* impenetrable, he thought, despite the fact that none of the bombs dropped earlier had been able to quiet its incessant firing. Bullets pulsating past his head were just inches away as he worked his way closer to his target. The rocks were sharp and they cut into him as he slithered over them, staying as low as possible. The sweat from his forehead rolled down into his eyes, the stinging salt forcing him to blink uncontrollably. Then, as he turned slightly to traverse a small mound of dirt, a bullet passed through his shoulder, ripping flesh and muscle as it tore its way through to daylight. The pain sent a vibrating agony through his entire body. He shuddered and closed his eyes tightly for a second before continuing on. The wound bled profusely, but nothing would stop him.

Now close enough to feel the heat from the flame of the gunpowder as it exploded, propelling the deadly bullets out of the gun, Owens rolled over on his back. From this vulnerable prone position he pulled the safety pin from a fragmentation grenade. He counted two beats then lobbed it backwards, up and over his head, into the heart of the bunker. The soldier firing the machine gun never saw it. The explosion blew him and his gun straight up into the air, filling him with hundreds of lethal fragments. Two other men in the bunker, upon seeing the grenade, tried to save themselves by leaping over the embankment. They barely made it out in time, but Owens, who had already rolled back onto his stomach into firing position, was prepared for them.

Before they had time to fire a single shot, he picked them off with just two rounds. After sixteen hours of hell, the deadly machine gun fell silent.

The other soldiers and their lieutenant in the trench raced to Owens' side. He was still on his stomach, relishing how quiet it had become. It was at that moment he realized he had just survived his own rash impulse to eliminate this enemy. And now that the mission had been accomplished and he started to collect his thoughts, the pain of the bullet that had passed through his shoulder registered in his brain. He let out a gasp of air and blacked out momentarily, face down in the dirt. The men he had just saved quickly carried him off.

Owens regained consciousness as the medic finished the temporary bandage in preparation for their return to their company and the hospital facilities. His life was no longer in danger. The lieutenant, kneeling beside him, informed him that Johnny Johnson, the soldier he had brought back to safety, had died, and that his last words were praise and gratitude for the man who'd risked his life for him.

The officer added, "I am recommending you for the Purple Heart because of your wound, but also the Medal of Honor for your bravery. You've earned it. You saved us all and I don't want that to ever be forgotten."

Dave Owens looked up at the lieutenant, squinting as rays of sunlight cut through the last vestige of fog. "I was just doing my job, Sir."

Iraq – September 2005

ANOTHER TYPICAL DAY one hundred miles east of Baghdad. Late afternoon had brought the temperature down to almost 100°, and the Tiger Trucking Company drivers, just back from their routes, were settling in for dinner. Dave Owens and the other new hire, Charlie Johnson, climbed out of an air-conditioned van, both recoiling as the heat hit them like a blast furnace. Owens looked around before his eyes settled on the driver, Tom Randall, the superintendent...and his new boss.

"This is where we're going to be living when not on the road?"

"You got it. The men call it Camp Mojave."

Johnson looked around. "Where's the bunk room...and it *is* air-conditioned, ain't it?"

"This is the building you'll be staying in. The other one is the kitchen and cook's quarters. Both have a lounge area...and yes, they are fully air-conditioned."

Owens couldn't help but think that his new home was a hellhole, a far cry from his secluded place in the mountains next to a cool stream filled with trout. One damn screw-up nine months ago and here he was, stuck in the middle of the desert for at least a year. Still, he wouldn't gripe about the living conditions. He had spent his entire life keeping his thoughts to himself. What other people didn't know about him couldn't be used against him. He had made his choices, now he had to live with them.

Charlie Johnson had his story too...devastated six months earlier when his high school sweetheart—wife, partner in business, bed and all of life for forty-five years— had died suddenly. This new trucker home sucked, just like his life now that she was gone. Normally jovial, a lot of that left with her. He was the first to get his suitcase from the back of the van. It landed with a thud on the dirt, almost pulling him down on top of it. It was big, just like him, and it was old and heavy...just like him.

One of the other drivers, Bud Tompkins, stuck his head outside the main building as the luggage mishap was taking place and called back to the rest of the group, "Wait till you see this." He laughed and shook his head in disbelief as he went back inside.

The dozen or so other drivers hurried to the windows to observe first-hand the groaning of the new hire as he wrestled with his luggage. "Where the hell did Randall find these two old geezers anyway?" Tompkins asked.

"From an old folks home maybe?" another said.

"Hey, Jacobs, Numley." Tompkins addressed two older men who hadn't bothered to get up from their chairs. "Looks like you got some new friends even older than you."

"We don't stock Metamucil here, so I sure hope these old farts brought their own."

"Maybe the shit will be scared out of 'em the first time they run into a terrorist." The last comment came from Butch

Simkins, who stood at the front of the group as Randall and the new hires walked in. Tall and muscular, he served as ringleader.

Randall introduced Owens and Johnson with some background on each. Owens, ex-military, had come out of retirement, and Johnson had been a professional truck driver in the states with a lot of big rig experience, something this crew lacked.

Simkins took a step forward, apprising the two new drivers. "First thing you'll want to do is get to know the other old drivers in the crew." He pointed toward the two men still seated. In a loud whisper that could be heard by everyone in the room he said, "The guy on the left, Jacobs, got booted out of his last job. Couldn't get hired on anywhere else, so we took 'em. The other guy is Numley. He got caught screwin' around on his wife and she kicked his ass out of the house. No place to go, we got stuck with him too."

Then he leaned in close to Owens…inches from his face. "This is a young man's job. Hope we don't have to spend extra time spoon feedin' you information about how to do it."

"Don't worry about us. Charlie and me can pull our own weight…"

Simkins hadn't waited for an answer. He'd already gone to get a cup of coffee.

Owens instantly decided he didn't care much for this guy Simkins. He knew the two of them would likely be exchanging more than just words in the next go-around unless the asshole changed his attitude.

Owens and Johnson were hired together. Both in their sixties, Owens, at sixty-four, was a bit older. They joined two other older men, both in their late fifties, who had been hired several months earlier. One of them, Rodney L. Numley, didn't even know how to drive a stick shift. The other, Keith Jacobs, had run an annuity sales force and also had no experience driving trucks. All four were hired after the trucking company won a lucrative contract from the new Iraqi government. No one knew if they were hired to meet mandatory diversity requirements or if they were the only ones available when the jobs were posted. The common denominator was they all needed to earn a lot of money in the shortest time possible. Working as a Wal-Mart greeter wouldn't cut it, so their solution was to drive a truck in Iraq.

Randall finished by reiterating, "Johnson here has more truck driving experience than all of you combined. Pick his brain when you can; it might make your job easier."

He turned to the new hires and laughed. "Watch out for these guys. They like to mess around with one another...especially the new men. Numley can attest to that."

With that, Randall returned to his van for the long drive back to Baghdad. In his late forties, he was tough enough to keep his crew of twenty and thirty year olds in line. He was respected...a boss who treated everyone fairly. His men called him a straight shooter, someone they could count on when the situation demanded it. Acting as mediator between the younger and older men, however, would be a real test for him. And unless the two groups made some concessions, he knew — like it or not — he would have to intervene. He empathized with the new men, which was why he warned them about the practical jokes. They were going to be the brunt of those jokes for a while. That alone could make their adjustment to the job more difficult, maybe cause some of them to not fulfill their one-year commitment.

All new drivers signed contracts, but some didn't even last a month. They had to work a full quarter or they would have to return their signing bonus. In addition, the cost of their roundtrip airfare would be deducted from their last paycheck. If they worked two quarters they earned a second bonus, bringing their pay up to over one hundred thousand dollars. And if they lasted the entire year it would top two hundred thousand dollars. The pay at Tiger Trucking was competitive. It had to be to compete against larger companies like Halliburton and the rest...not to mention the risks involved.

Most of the men had their reasons for being in Iraq, and it was usually money. Of course, some just wanted to experience the excitement, something they could brag about back home. Those were usually the young, often immature single men. Whatever the reason, Camp Mojave was staffed by many different personality types, all thrown together. It amazed corporate that there weren't more fights. Probably because of one common denominator: it was the good guys against the bad guys, Americans against insurgents and terrorists. Otherwise, they would probably need to supply a full-time physician rather than employ the current practice of first-aid training for the cooks.

The new men were now on their own, Randall figured as he drove off. He hoped they would make it. He chuckled as he said out loud, "At least for the next several months, so I can make my quotas."

ℜ

Owens and Johnson gravitated to the other two older drivers.

Numley stuck out his hand to greet them and blurted, "My reason for being here isn't exactly the way Butch said."

"Don't worry about it," Owens responded, "we've all got our unpleasant reasons as to why we're here. When we have some free time you can catch us up if you want to."

Johnson said, "Hey Rod, what did Randall mean when he said you knew all about these guys messing around with people?"

Numley scowled. "It's Rodney, and it was bad. It happened just after I got here. I had to take a shit and asked where the john was. Tompkins said it was out back…a hot, dirty old Porta-Potty."

Keith Jacobs started laughing. "Looking back on it now, you've got to admit it *was* funny."

"Funny my ass. I was locked in that shithole for over twenty minutes before he found me and let me out."

Jacobs added, "We discovered later it was Tompkins and Lewis who locked the door and blocked the air vent."

"There wasn't any toilet paper either. It stunk so bad I got sick in there."

"Sick? He reeked from the smell of shit and his own puke."

"I had to strip down and hose off outside before they'd let me back in here. They said it was a rite of passage."

Butch Simpkins, overhearing the conversation, said, "I told you not to take it so personal, Numley. Everyone gets their turn." Then he leered at Owens. "And I do mean *everyone*."

Owens took a couple of steps forward. "Let me put it this way...*Butch*: we've only been here a few minutes and you've already managed to piss me off. If I were you I'd stop while I was ahead. Understood?"

Simkins maintained his arrogant facade, looking around to make sure he was still backed by his dozen men. "No sweat. It's all in fun around here. No harm, no foul. Your room is down the hall, just past the bathroom...the indoor one."

They all laughed.

ℜ

Butch Simkins—given name Leon—had grown up in a small town where he had always been a bully, probably because he'd been the biggest kid in class since the first grade. By junior high he had already started drinking and smoking marijuana, and was one of a handful of students drunk at his graduation. He never did graduate from high school, dropping out at seventeen.

At the age of thirty, Simkins wasn't much farther along in life than he had been when he dropped out of school. Menial jobs, little money. Then, finding himself in a situation where he needed to leave town for a while, a couple of friends told him about a chance to earn some big bucks for a year's work in Iraq: a perfect solution.

Butch Simkins looked forward to the fun he would have with the new hires, even though he had a problem with the one named Owens. Old, yeah, but he could tell, one tough son of a bitch.

ℜ

The trucker camp stood in the middle of the desert by corporate design to provide greater safety for its occupants. But located so far out, cell phones were inoperable. When the men were in camp, they had to take turns using the one available landline…when it was working.

One advantage of this location was its distance from the deadly Sunni Triangle, well known as the most dangerous place in the entire country. The triangle, in the heart of Iraq, went from Tikrit south to Baghdad, west to Ramadi then north back up to Tikrit. Saddam Hussein received most of his support from this area when he was in power. Being over a hundred miles east of Baghdad left it far from the explosions that killed soldiers and Iraqi citizens on a daily basis in the triangle. There wasn't much for the drivers to do in Baghdad anyway, so it didn't really matter to them where the camp was. They normally drove five to six days a week, starting their weekend—such as it was—as early on Saturday as they could.

The geography was stark: what growth existed looked like scrub brush from the deserts in the United States, with an occasional tree, hence the name Camp Mojave, after the high desert in California. Temperatures would top 120° much of the year. Sand, however, was worse than the heat. It was very fine and got into everything. Continual coughing and sneezing could be heard day and night. And there were the constant sandstorms, at least every other week or so.

Hellhole pretty much described Camp Mojave.

Day One – Saturday, January 7, 2006

THE LOUNGE stood ready for the traditional Saturday night poker game. Dave Owens and Charlie Johnson had been on board for four months, Keith Jacobs and Rodney Numley seven months. The *old guys*, as they were now referred to by the younger drivers, had endured occasional pranks and had made the adjustment to a different way of life unscathed. The two age groups had grown used to each other and got along well, considering their differences. The only exception was Butch Simkins and his buddies, Tompkins and Lewis, who took every opportunity to make life more difficult for the older drivers.

Richard Murdock, a transportation and storage consultant, had been in camp for the past week to ride with each driver, observing their daily routines and probing for cost-cutting ideas. Although he had not yet been officially invited to play, the younger drivers were especially excited about the game, as they knew they had a new well-heeled player in Murdock. They planned to take a lot of his money.

A chance to win fresh money was important; many bet their entire paychecks during a game, then found themselves tapped out for half a month until payday. The losers were usually bitter, and showed it, often with temper tantrums. In their first game the old guys had won big. They were never invited to play after that. They either watched the game, read a book or occasionally set up their own game in one of their bunkrooms. The pots in the big game were often too steep for them anyway. Their goal was to earn — and keep — a lot of money. They thought the kids were crazy to bet so much money in a stupid card game.

The old guys had decided the previous day to use the cook's quarters this particular evening to set up their own game away from the other drivers and their bullshit. The cooks always had Saturday night off. The place would be theirs, including access to the refrigerators with leftover food for a midnight snack. Owens and Numley left right after dinner, Jacobs not far behind. Johnson would join them when he returned from the day's route.

ℜ

Charlie Johnson had been one of the four drivers assigned to work that day. He felt thankful it was only one Saturday a month. Although he wasn't as tired at the end of a week as he was when he first arrived, he still enjoyed a two-day weekend to rest up from the limited amount of lifting required by the job that still wasn't appreciated by his tired old body. He was now in better condition thanks to Dave Owens and his insistence that all the older men participate in physical training exercises several days a week. As motivation, Owens had told them how it would make their job easier and that he personally knew of older men who had survived heart attacks just because they had been in better than normal physical condition due to regular exercise. Easier or not, Johnson still had it tougher than the others as he had to lift on one short leg, the result of childhood polio. The only good thing about that disease, aside from surviving it, was that it exempted him from the draft; he never had to go to Vietnam like his brother did.

His normal day started about 6:30 a.m.; but he was usually back in camp by six p.m., in time for dinner. Johnson rarely missed dinner, or any other meal for that matter, if he could help it. He admitted that he liked to eat, which was why his 5'10" frame weighed over 230 pounds. When friends expressed concern about his weight he would merely say that at his age it didn't much matter. He was closer to death than life anyway, so he might as well enjoy what was left. His personality had grown on old and young alike, now one of the most likeable men in camp, with a twinkle in his eyes as if about to tell a joke — which he did more often than not. That day he couldn't help but think about the card game he and the others had just planned for this evening, and he could hardly wait to get back to camp.

Living here and doing this job was not something Johnson thought he would ever have to endure. The trucks they drove were primarily four-, six- and ten-wheelers that could carry fairly large loads. The one eighteen-wheeler was huge in comparison to most of the other trucks. When the big rig was needed, he was the only driver that could handle it effectively. As many of the streets were extremely narrow, it was seldom used. The smaller trucks were more practical and easier to navigate when they got into some of the towns to pick up and deliver crates of food and other consumable household products. They were also easier to drive by men with less experience, which included most of the ones working out of Camp Mojave. This lack of experience was yet another reason the fleet consisted mostly of gasoline-powered trucks rather than diesel.

Johnson arrived at the western Baghdad warehouse as scheduled to pick up his first load of merchandise, only to learn it wasn't ready. It still needed to be sorted and crated. In addition, the professional shooter assigned to his truck to provide protection while he was on the road could not be found. That in itself was disturbing, as these specialists were sometimes tracked down and killed by terrorists to eliminate yet another perceived threat. Management took over three hours to find him a replacement. As it was against the rules to venture out onto the streets of Iraq without a shooter, the truck could not be dispatched. Company policy was company policy. But with roadside bombings killing far more drivers than those that had been attacked by terrorists or insurgents, the thought of which scared the hell out of Charlie Johnson, he never fully understood the value of the mandatory bodyguard. He guessed that, if he were attacked, he would be grateful for this added protection, and he thanked God he had never been subjected to either an assault or a bombing attempt, which was just fine with him. The daily tension he felt on the job wasn't diminished in the least, with or without a shooter on board.

While waiting for a shooter, Johnson thought about the people that the company hired to protect them. Private professional guards were expensive due to the tremendous amount of risk involved for anyone authorized to carry a weapon. These highly trained gunmen were paid up to $600 per day for a regular job. If they were protecting someone important, with high visibility, the pay could be as much as $1,000 per day or even more, depending upon the circumstances. Other than the military, these guards were the only non-Iraqi personnel allowed to legally carry a firearm within the borders of Iraq.

Even after the load was separated and ready, Johnson had to wait another two hours for his guard. By the time he got back on the road he was over three hours behind, with no way to make it up. It was going to be a long Saturday after all. He would miss dinner, but maybe he could catch the end of the card game.

ℜ

After dinner, Keith Jacobs had decided to finish putting away his freshly laundered clothes before joining the game. In one corner of a drawer he saw the red, white and blue scarf Lynn had sent him the previous week. He smiled, remembering that his wife had said she was going to learn how to knit while he was away. He doubted it would ever be cold enough to wear the scarf in Iraq, and he also knew that displaying the American colors wasn't the brightest thing anyone could do while on the road. It only took one pissed-off Iraqi to ruin a driver's day. He loved it though and could hardly wait to put it on. Probably when he got home.

It was while admiring the scarf that he heard Butch Simkins' loud voice out in the hall telling him they needed a big pot of coffee for the card game. He scowled. Simkins was the asshole of the bunch, and unlike the other men had never really accepted the old guys. He had been a problem since the first day they arrived. One of the nastier confrontations flashed through Jacobs' mind as he put his last article of clothing away. It had taken place a week after they'd arrived at camp.

Butch had staggered into the lounge, obviously drunk, showing off a gun he carried in his boot, a secret to everyone except the other truckers in the camp. He'd twirled the pistol on his index finger, then pointed it at Numley and slurred, "Bang bang, you're dead."

His shrill voice was even more obnoxious because of the drinking. "If any of those chicken-shit terrorists give me a bad time, they're gonna have a fight on their hands. They may get me, but I'll take a few of 'em with me…with this!"

He spun the weapon on his finger again and staggered around the room, waving it in a broad circle.

"This here is an American made Smith & Wesson 357 magnum with a three-inch barrel. I can easily hit a target up to fifteen yards away. That's because I'm a highly trained marksman."

He pointed to a notch on the handle. "It's killed once and it'll kill again if anyone gets in my way. It's a bad-ass weapon, let me tell ya."

He aimed the gun at Charlie Johnson and said, "It would even go through that big gut of yours, old man."

Johnson held up his hands as Dave Owens walked into the room. He glared at Simkins, who took a step back.

"Quit screwing around and put that damn gun away...*now*," Owens snapped. "They have a habit of going off by accident, and none of us want to be here when it does."

"Hey, no worries," Simkins replied. "Everything's under control."

"You don't have anything under control, you asshole; you're drunk. Go sleep it off."

Simkins clenched a fist and started toward Owens, but immediately thought better about it. While chewing hard on the toothpick he always had in his mouth, he slowly bent over and put the gun back in his boot. To save face he muttered, "I've had enough fun with you old farts for one day anyway." He turned and left the room.

No one had ever confronted Simkins before. Pride swelled up in the other old guys. One of their own had effectively handled the most intimidating guy in camp. Their self-esteem started to return. They all did the same job, but Simkins thought he and the younger drivers did it better; and that the older guys were their servants. Making coffee for a card game was just one example. This positive turn of events after just one week helped make their life more enjoyable with everyone...except Butch and his two cronies.

ℜ

Jacobs walked into the lounge area and was surprised to see his boss there at this late hour on a Saturday. Richard Murdock, the consultant, stood by Randall as he spoke with the younger drivers.

"So with that in mind, Murdock will stay on a bit longer to finish riding with the rest of you. He's already collected a lot of valuable information and I want to make sure we get everyone's suggestions. It's not a waste of time; I'm already figuring out how to use some of your ideas. If you want to complain about things, go for it. Negative responses will not have anybody's name attached, so be as candid as you want. You will, however, get credit for any positive ideas we use. Any questions?"

Silence.

"Good. And let's continue to treat Mr. Murdock here like a VIP while he's with us. If this works the way I expect, his efforts will yield a lot of improvements."

"Did I miss anything important?" Jacobs asked as he joined the group.

"Keith. You already know Richard Murdock, right?" Randall asked.

"Yep. He's been here all week. I wondered if he was going to ride with me?"

"Yes, next week. He's staying on until he rides with everyone."

"Great." Jacobs looked at Murdock and added, "We're inside now. Do you ever take off your flak jacket and steel helmet? I don't think I've ever seen you without them on!"

Murdock laughed. "I keep them on at all times…even when I go to bed. Especially when I go to bed. That's when we're most vulnerable."

Jacobs agreed with him about their vulnerability, then invited him to join the old guys for their card game. Murdock said, "I play a lot of bridge, but I assume you're talking about poker?"

"Yeah, all the different games, even Texas Hold 'Em."

Simkins immediately interrupted, explaining to Murdock that the big money game would be there in the lounge. "You can stay right here and play…unless big stakes are a problem."

"Not at all. I think I can handle the pressure."

Jacobs shrugged and started to leave, then told Murdock, "If the stakes get too high or the conversation too raunchy, there'll be an empty chair for you across the way."

"Thanks, I'll be by later. I just need a little time to win all their money first before coming over to get yours."

After the laugh, Randall said, "Men, I want everyone to be especially alert this next week. Before I left Baghdad, the base commander called. One of his informants told him there was going to be an attack on civilians by one of the al-Qaeda cells. He didn't know where, but that it could take place at any time. We doubt it would be way out here, but be careful anyway."

Randall left. Jacobs noticed Simkins patting his boot. He shook his head. Macho Man probably figured he could take out a whole cell by himself. Asshole.

ℜ

Richard Murdock was a *true* VIP, having been sent to Iraq by the U.S. government. He'd accepted the request as a sense of duty to his country as well as a favor to his good friend, the vice president. He had started his own successful transportation company over a decade earlier and was now wealthy, the result of selling it the prior year. As a front he was a consultant for the trucking companies. In fact, he was there to help Iraq set up regulations for its own storage and transportation industry. His assignment, as part of the Coalition Provisional Authority, was to study their existing capabilities and recommend improvements during a six-month stay. What was indeed remarkable was that Murdock had agreed to help out at great personal risk, not to mention horrible living conditions compared to his lifestyle at home.

By any measure he was highly successful, and yet only in his late forties. Six feet tall, he was heavyset and intimidating in stature but his eyes hinted at perpetual humor. To the younger men he was more a father figure than the grandfatherly old guys, and therefore more acceptable to them. Nearly bald, he sported a full beard about an inch in length. He was quick-witted, connecting easily with people. This skill helped him to quickly extract information he needed for his work.

Murdock lived on a large, beautiful ranch in Colorado. In Iraq, he found himself in a two-room prefab building on the grounds adjacent to the Baghdad airport, sharing the rooms, complete with one bath and small shower, with three other men. They survived on next to no conveniences whatsoever. The only amenity was a small window air conditioning unit that ran when they had electricity, which was only some of the time. Here was a man with everything, risking his life to help his country establish a free and prosperous Iraq.

ℜ

The men opened their cans of beer, got some snacks, and sat down around the table. Simkins dealt the first hand. He told Murdock to make himself comfortable, that he could even take off his protective armor. He assured him that they were perfectly safe with the guards patrolling the grounds outside. They were so safe, he said, they didn't even have to turn off their lights at nine like other trucker camps were forced to do because the others were located closer to Baghdad.

"You said you liked cards...your main hobby then?" Simkins asked.

Murdock shook his head. "I've got a lot of hobbies, like flying planes, something I do whenever I get the chance. And I love to travel and visit museums in other countries."

He explained that the museums coincided with his real interest: ancient artifacts that spoke so loud and clear about historical events. He had made a lifelong study of this. He reminded them about the looting that took place in Baghdad before and after the invasion...that priceless and ir-replaceable items had been stolen. His concern was that they might be lost to humanity forever. He showed them a list of the missing pieces he carried with him, just in case he stumbled onto any of it.

"I hope someone recovers these items in one piece. It will be a tremendous loss if they aren't found!"

Butch, not really caring, replied, "Yeah...a real loss. Now then, how much do you want to bet?"

ℜ

Colonel Abdul, supervisor of the guards, walked the perimeter of the camp, as he did every evening, making sure his young Iraqi guards were exactly where they were supposed to be. He had learned years ago to *inspect what you expect* to minimize the number of times he would be disappointed by his subordinates.

Even though Iraq's first couple of free elections had taken place and the new government was starting to assume most of the control of their country, scores of people continued to be killed by suicide bombers dedicated to the cause of martyrdom, or forced to participate because members of their family had been taken hostage and would be tortured and killed if they didn't cooperate. Al-Qaeda operatives also continued to kidnap and publicly kill American workers, Iraqi citizens and anyone else they thought were sympathetic to the new regime. The locals, still afraid, stood idly by watching death and destruction all around them. They wanted the terrorists from surrounding countries to leave and let them solve their own problems. They thought the Iraqi insurgents were misguided monsters as they continued to destroy their own country. They knew both groups had an agenda, and that it wasn't safe for anyone in their sights.

Unlike the professional shooters that rode with the drivers, corporate headquarters, as a cost-cutting measure, had hired a handful of local Iraqi civilians for pennies a day to guard the camp around the clock. The drivers all knew they were amateurs, that the only guard with any combat experience was their supervisor, Colonel Abdul. He was responsible for hiring, training, and assigning them their duties. The guards called him Aag-eed, Arabic for colonel, and they idolized him. He encouraged them as a mentor. When they made mistakes—which was often—he would assure them they were learning together, that they would do better the next time. He was like a second father to them.

One of the newest guards, Jabaar, perhaps from the poorest family of the lot, had been surprised to learn that their training only took one day. They were taught how to march in order, which they were told was very important, and how to load and fire their M-16 assault rifles. They were directed to shoot anyone trying to enter the camp without proper identification. Although young and innocent in the ways of the world, the guards were all proud of their opportunity to help protect Americans who had freed their country and were helping to rebuild it. The lives of the truckers, however, depended upon the ability of these young guards to detect a problem and neutralize it before it became a deadly reality. The question was, were they up to the task?

This Saturday night was especially dark. The guards could barely see a thing as they patrolled the camp. Colonel Abdul quietly approached one of them, and was finally observed from just a few feet away. The guard, as trained, pointed his rifle at his supervisor and shouted, "Halt. Who goes there?"

Abdul responded with a *well done*. He told him it was his Aag-eed, just making sure everything was going well that evening. He asked if the guard had noticed anything suspicious.

"Aag-eed. Thank Allah it is you. Nothing suspicious, sir. We are all a little more nervous tonight because it is so dark."

"Stay alert. If you can't see out here, neither can they, so we aren't at any disadvantage. I'll see you in the morning."

Colonel Abdul disappeared into the dark as he continued his inspection tour…his actions watched closely through night-vision binoculars from a nearby hilltop.

ℜ

Ali Salim, al-Qaeda cell leader and organizer of the attack, put the binoculars back in their case and signaled his minions to take their positions. After months of planning, his most sought-after goal was finally being realized.

The first hooded attacker crawled silently through the underbrush that surrounded the camp, stalking his victim. Neutralizing the nearest peripheral guard was his objective.

He had his AK-47 in one hand, an eleven-inch knife with its high carbon steel and partially serrated edge blade in the other. The guard stopped moving as he stared out into the darkness, listening intently for any suspicious sounds.

The hooded man, now within a few feet of his quarry, quietly put his rifle on the ground and grasped the knife firmly in his right hand. As the guard started to move on, the attacker pounced on his back, covering his mouth with his left hand, using it to quickly pull his head backward. The blade of the knife found the guard's exposed neck, slicing through his jugular vein and windpipe all the way to the vertebrae. The guard slumped to the ground, a gurgling sound emanating from his throat before dying in seconds. One by one the other guards around the perimeter of the camp met the same fate.

After the dead bodies were hidden in nearby brush, the attackers took up their position at two windows on one side of the room where the Americans played cards. Two were already stationed at the windows on the other side of the building. After killing the first guard, the hooded intruder approached the guard at the front door of the main quarters. The goal was the same: to quickly kill him before attacking the men inside. Ali had already positioned himself at the back door. The guard was eliminated in the same fashion as the others, swiftly and silently. Eleven p.m. They were now ready for their main thrust.

ℜ

The terrorists had worked closely with a trucking company employee, an informant who had positioned himself to provide them with invaluable information in preparation for the assault. This man entered the main quarters, knowing the attack was only minutes away, and took up a position next to the strongest of the group...the man with the gun. He glanced at the new consultant, knowing his arrival meant one more American to get even with. It was then he realized the older drivers were missing.

"Where are the other men?" he asked.

Simkins said, "You mean the old farts? They decided to have their own game over at the cook's quarters. This here is a man's game...you know that."

The informant nodded, knowing the attackers would have to go over to the other building when they were done here. Every American in the camp would be captured or killed. No one would escape.

The card game, by this time, had grown serious. Murdock wasn't the card-playing pushover the younger drivers had anticipated. The current hand was down to him and Simkins, with cards that told him this was finally his turn to win a big one.

Murdock looked up from his cards and said, "Old farts? Are you talking about Keith and his friends? They seem OK to me."

"Wait till you get to know them like I have. They're kinda slow on the uptake. I think you'll want to ride with the men in this room next week and forget about them."

"Thanks for the warning, Butch, but I'll make that decision on my own. Now then…it's down to you and me and it's a big pot. Show me what you've got. I call."

Simkins quickly turned over his cards, almost laughing as he did so. "A full house…three jacks and two nines. Read em and weep!"

With a somber look, Murdock started to slowly turn over his cards. Simkins figured he had finally won a hand.

Murdock said, "Pretty good, Butch, but not quite good enough. I've got a full house too, but all of my cards have faces smiling up at me!"

"Damn." Simkins shrugged. "That's the third big pot you've won. And I thought tonight was going to be lucky. Deal 'em again —"

A deafening roar filled the room as both doors and all four windows flew open with a burst of gunfire. The drivers hit the floor, stunned by the sound of the AK-47 assault rifles, purchased long ago from communist supporters in Russia.

The masked attackers entered the room simultaneously with one of them shouting in broken English, "Stay down with eyes shut or get shot!"

One of the youngest drivers, drunk and daring, lunged at him snarling, "Screw you!"

Ali put four bullets in him, dropping him before he even got close. "No, screw you!"

As he lay on the floor writhing in pain while taking his last gulp of air, the informant knocked Simkins unconscious and retrieved his hidden pistol. Only Murdock noticed. But there was nothing he could do about it. He knew from his training that, for now, all he could do was obey their orders and stall for time, hoping help would arrive before it was too late.

℣

The hooded men had missed the newly hired Iraqi guard, Jabaar, as he stood in the shadows of the cook's quarters. He had left his post to smoke a cigarette, purposely cupping it in his hand so Colonel Abdul wouldn't see it if he looked out a window. He had witnessed the noise and flame from the blazing guns during the violent attack on the main quarters without being observed. Fortunately for the old guys, the terrorists had missed them as well; they had been informed that everyone would be in the main building. The three men heard the shots and jumped to their feet.

"What the hell. That sounds like AK-47s!" Owens shouted.

Jabaar raced in by the back door and signaled everyone to be quiet.

"What's going on out there?" Owens asked. "It sounds like a war."

"Terrorists," the guard whispered in broken English. "They already inside main building. Don't know if everybody shot or not…it happen fast."

"We've got to get out of here, or we'll be next!" Jacobs exclaimed.

"Back door only hope," Jabaar said. "Closest way to hills and rocks. Got rifle, but it only one gun against many."

"Let's go!" Owens took charge. "Grab the water. We'll figure out what to do after we're out of here."

They scooped up the three bottles of water that had been sitting on the table and sprinted for the back door. Reaching the nearby foliage, they quickly plunged into it. As fast as they could in the dark, they ran up the hill overlooking the camp to hide behind the rocks and determine their next course of action. How fortunate that there was no moon that night. They would be difficult to find in the dark, and it just might save their lives.

ℜ

One by one, the men were bound with duct tape. The body of the dead driver had already been rolled out of the way. The flak jacket and steel helmet worn by Murdock were roughly removed before he was bound.

"You think that would protect you from us?" Ali sneered as he shook his head in disgust. "The armor of Allah is all we need."

After tying their hands behind their backs, the attackers taped their eyes and mouths. They were not to see or say anything until they were far away and safely hidden.

Not one of the surviving men offered any resistance. They had been taken by surprise and there had never been any preparation on the part of the company about what to do in an event like this. It wasn't supposed to happen way out here. From the attackers' perspective, everything was going according to plan.

The informant waited until the main building was secure, the drivers all bound and gagged, before mentioning the older men. "They are probably hiding in the closets, pissing their pants and hoping we don't know they even exist," he said.

Ali told his men, "When you find them, bring them here so they can meet the same fate as their infidel friends."

The hooded attackers smashed through the front door of the cook's quarters to find it empty. The other Americans were nowhere to be found, not even in the closets, as the informant had thought. Assuming they'd fled out the back door, they followed in hopes of finding them hiding nearby. They even fired a few shots, thinking the infidels might reveal themselves by gasping in fear. They heard nothing. Not even the probing arcs of their flashlights could find them.

"They are on foot. With what we have planned, they will die tomorrow anyway. Let's get back to the others. We still have more work to do."

Now past midnight, they needed to leave with their prisoners as quickly as possible. They herded them outside and loaded them in the back of the truck they had selected for the job. The exit plan was designed to evade the American investigators who would ultimately come looking for them.

While two of the attackers stayed behind, the others jumped aboard the truck and drove it down the dirt road a few miles to the main highway that led to Baghdad. Within a mile they pulled over to the side of the highway and cut brush so the truck could get off and double back. The brush was replaced, making the area look just as it had before the truck passed through. Additional brush was tied to the back of the truck, erasing its tire tracks as it sped to another dirt road on the other side of the small hill near camp.

"They will think we have taken the prisoners back to Baghdad. The infidel fools will never figure out the truth."

Everything had been well thought out.

ℜ

Charlie Johnson was now midway through one of his worst days since arriving in Iraq. Although the road ahead appeared to be wide open, he crawled behind the slow-moving truck of a competitor. He had spoken to the driver, a likeable guy, at the last stop, but now he traveled so slowly that Johnson had decided about a mile back to pass him at the first opportunity. His truck was smaller and more maneuverable. And he *was* running behind schedule. It would also impress the customer if he could arrive ahead of his competitor.

The road finally widened enough for Johnson to pass. But as he swung out to go around the other truck, he noticed that the street had become crowded with pedestrians. He made a split second decision not to pass, just in case one of them happened to dart out into the road. He definitely did not want to hit anyone, especially not in *this* country.

As he slowed down and pulled back into his own lane, a sudden and unbelievably large flash followed by a thunderous roar erupted in front of him. He watched in horror as it vaporized the nearby pedestrians and flipped the truck in front of him on its side. He slammed on his brakes and leaped from his vehicle, running as fast as his old body would let him to try and help the other driver.

By the time he reached the big rig's cab, it was already engulfed in flames. The intensity of its heat kept him at bay. He shouted, "Buddy, are you still in there? Can you get out? Talk to me!"

He immediately knew the answer. He was just close enough to hear the agonizing screams of the driver. The ensuing explosion of the truck's fuel tank, located just behind the cab, quieted him forever.

Johnson, unscathed by the second explosion, bowed his shaking head in sorrow. "Why do people do things like this anyway?" he said to no one in particular, knowing that by the grace of God he had narrowly missed being the victim of this disaster. His body shuddered as he thought about it. This just as easily could have been him, not his competitor.

The military arrived within minutes and Johnson described what he had seen in as much detail as he could remember, calming his nerves with a big bite of chaw. He then climbed into his truck and continued on to the customer, badly shaken, knowing his competitor would never reach this destination.

It was now well past dark when he arrived at his final stop. The two men assigned to offload his truck before he returned to Camp Mojave had already left, and now his shooter did the same.

"Mr. Charlie," the shop owner said, "you must wait until morning for men to come back."

This meant he would have to sleep either in the back room of the owner's store or in his own truck. Neither idea had much appeal. He was still on the western outskirts of Baghdad, way too close to all the killings for anyone in their right mind to be spending the night.

"I can unload the truck myself. Can you keep your dock open til I get it done?"

The owner agreed to accommodate *Mr. Charlie,* but the normal thirty-minute job took almost two hours, and the only reason it didn't take longer was because the owner finally helped out toward the end, as he too wanted to go home.

Bitter disappointment was an understatement as Johnson finally headed back to camp in his now empty truck. He had not only missed dinner, but the much anticipated card game as well. Way past midnight, he knew the others would already be asleep. The younger ones would still be playing cards in the lounge and whooping it up, probably all drunk. Many of them would also be broke until next payday. He hoped the new guy, Murdock, had taken everybody's money. It would serve them right.

Johnson left the paved highway still thinking about the devastating roadside bombing that had taken place right in front of him. As he entered the dirt road that led toward camp he turned to a more pleasant thought: raiding the cook's quarters for some leftovers from dinner before falling into his bunk. At last, one very bad day in his life was finally over.

ℜ

The explosion had been timed to take place after the terrorists and their prisoners were several miles down the road. Bright red and orange flames burst skyward as the blasts obliterated everything in the camp. The ground shook as if caused by a massive earthquake. The old guys were the only ones who witnessed all of this from the hill.

"Can you believe this?" Numley said.

"It's like some kind of nightmare," Keith Jacobs replied.

From their position before the explosion they had observed the activity in the camp as best they could in the dark. They had seen the intruders with their flashlights enter the building they had just vacated, then watched in terror as they came running out the back, plunging through the bushes toward them. They flinched in silence each time a terrorist fired his rifle; they froze as beams of light sought them out.

Later they watched their captured comrades being loaded into one of the mid-size trucks with a canvas tarp over the top and down its sides, then driven off on the dirt road toward the Baghdad highway.

Numley whispered, "Did you see that? They used my truck to carry them away. Why *my* truck?"

"Didn't you say your gas gauge was broken?" Owens asked.

"Yes. It says the tank is full, but it's almost empty, probably less than a quarter of a tank. It's been broken for weeks now. The engine sputters over bumps too. I needed to fill out a form to get it fixed, but hadn't gotten around to it yet."

"Then they won't be driving far, will they?"

"Probably not. They'll wish they filled up instead of trusting that gauge. That'll surprise 'em, won't it?"

Once the truck had driven off, they watched two men that had remained behind run around the camp searching for…something.

"Maybe they're looking for us?"

Owens elbowed Numley, putting his finger to his lips for him to be quiet.

A few minutes later, apparently satisfied, the terrorists ran up the hill in the direction of the old guys.

"Shit, they're headed our way," Jacobs whispered. "Now what?"

"Quiet!" Owens snapped. "Jabaar, give me your rifle."

The two terrorists continued to run toward them. Thirty yards away, twenty-five, then twenty. Owens released the safety. At fifteen yards from the large rocks hiding the old guys, he inched upward into firing position. At that moment, both men veered off to their right and started down the other side of the hill. Only then did Owens dare to breathe.

The two terrorists reached the bottom of the hill. There, they were met by Numley's truck, which had circled back for them.

"Where'd that come from? Is there another road out here?" Owens asked.

"Yes…narrow dirt road," Jabaar said.

"Where does it go?"

"Iran. Mountain border."

"Damn it. They're taking them to *Iran?*"

Jacobs shrugged. "Clever, the way they've done it. Nobody would know if we hadn't seen it."

As the truck disappeared behind the far hill, the earth-shattering roar of the explosion jolted everyone. Numley, who had just stood up to stretch his legs, was thrown to the ground as the camp fuel tank blew, sending orange plumes high into the sky. Debris from buildings and trucks flew hundreds of feet into the air. Virtually everything in camp was demolished. Now they understood what the two remaining terrorists had been doing.

"What do we do now, Dave?" Numley asked. "We don't have anything. How do we survive?"

"Stay cool. We've got some water, and Charlie should be showing up before long."

"And we've got it easy compared to those guys." Jacobs gestured over his shoulder in the direction of the departing truck.

"Maybe we should start walking toward the highway," Numley said. "Charlie or somebody will eventually come by and pick us up."

Owens glared at him. "If the wrong people come by we could be shot, or worse…captured and tortured. Are you willing to take that chance? I'm not!"

They quickly decided not to attempt reaching Baghdad on foot. They needed to rely on Charlie and his truck to get them to safety. As they discussed alternatives, they saw lights coming down the dirt road from the highway.

"That's got to be Charlie now," Jacobs said. "He's the only one who would be coming out here at this hour."

They ran down the hill, staying low behind bushes just in case it wasn't their friend. They reached the road at the same time the truck came to a sudden stop.

Charlie opened the door and gasped. "What the hell?"

The small group of survivors, relieved to see their friend, approached him. "Charlie, it's us," Numley said. "The camp was attacked."

"No shit." He looked around and asked, "Where are the others?"

"Captured…all of them. They're headed toward Iran. We have to get to Baghdad and let 'em know what's happened out here."

"No can do."

"Why not?" Owens asked.

"Because I was running so late, I couldn't gas up in Baghdad. Everything was closed. I'm not running on fumes, but almost."

"How far do you think this truck can go?"

"Maybe another fifty or sixty miles. *Maybe.*"

"Damn. That would leave us in the middle of the desert if we tried to reach Baghdad...and no telling who we'd find lurking along that desolate stretch of road."

Owens considered their alternatives. They could stay here, but that might be risky. Other terrorists could come along and kill them or take them prisoner. Even if that didn't happen, what would they do for water or food?

"Charlie, do you have any food and water in your truck?"

"Just some beef jerky. I've also got some water left, but not a lot. There are tools in here too."

"Good, we might need them."

"What do you mean we might need them?" Numley asked. "What are you thinking about?"

They were the only ones who knew the captives had been taken toward the Iranian border instead of Baghdad. Owens figured that they were the only ones who could possibly help if—and that was a big *if*—they could discover where the prisoners were being held. Even so, the terrorists had a big head start on them.

If they did go after them, Owens was also concerned about the loyalties of Jabaar. He could disappear at any time and leave them stranded in the desert. Or worse, lead them into a trap if he were a sympathizer. Owens knew he would have to keep an eye on him.

"As I see it," he said, " we only have one choice. We can't go back, and we can't stay here. We have to follow them. It's the only chance those men have...and the best chance *we* have to survive."

"Are you kidding me?" Numley exclaimed. "They'll kill us too! Why don't we just wait here? Someone is bound to show up when they don't hear from us. We can ration the water. We'll make it."

"It's the weekend. They may not know we're missing until late Monday. We might be able to survive that long, but what about the others? Could you live with that? We don't have a choice. We've got to go after them."

"Then what? We catch up to them, then what do we do?"

"I don't know...but we'll figure it out. One step at a time."

Jacobs shook his head. "I don't know about this. There are so many unknowns. It sounds too risky."

"You're scared, OK. So am I. Anyone with any brains would be. But all I've heard from you guys for the past two months is your bitching and moaning about losing your jobs. You've *acted* like losers. Well, now's your chance to be men again. My gut tells me it's the right thing to do...the *only* thing to do. Are you with me...or not? Because I'm going after them no matter what you decide."

No reply, only dead silence. They had all seen what happened to other Americans that had been captured by these madmen. When demands weren't met—and they never were—they were beheaded. It was a gruesome ending for the innocent victims of this misguided radical Muslim cause. The captured drivers weren't the most mature guys in the world—kids, really—but they were Americans, and this time these ruthless bastards weren't going to get away with another atrocity. Not if Dave Owens had anything to say about it.

"Those of you who are with me, we've got to get going, and I mean right now!"

Johnson smiled. "Looks like old *DO* is back. I'm with you, partner." He jumped back into his truck and started it.

"I go too!" Jabaar said.

Not wanting to be left alone in the desert, Jacobs and Numley reluctantly agreed to join him as well.

Owens quickly scribbled a note, leaving it on one of the few poles still standing for anyone who came out to investigate. It was brief and to the point:

Terrorists headed toward Iran with captives.
We are following them.
Dave Owens

Charlie Johnson, told of the other road, had backtracked to the highway in order to circumvent the hill and take up pursuit of the other truck. Now he drove like a madman over the winding dirt road in an effort to lessen the gap between them and the terrorists, before their own truck ran out of gas. Even at that, their speed was limited due to the severe bends in the narrow road.

This part of the plan was delicate. If the terrorists detected them before they were prepared with some idea for a rescue attempt, they too would become hostages, or worse. They needed to get close enough without being seen so they could follow them to their destination. Only then would they be able to develop a more comprehensive rescue plan.

Lost in thought and racing through darkness, the last remaining bomb exploded. Owens' hastily written note instantly ignited into flames. They were now on their own without any hope of help.

℞

Smuggling the captured Americans over the border into Iran was a tactical part of the plan originated by Ali Salim. He knew they wouldn't be found by anyone, especially not the American forces. And even if they did, he knew they would be hesitant to try to do anything about it. Not on that side of the border, and especially not this particular country where their government, in defiance of the U.N. Security Council, had admitted they were resuming their conversion enrichment and reprocessing of uranium to continue their development of nuclear power, and it was feared, their own nuclear weapon.

It had always been part of the plan to destroy the camp to make it more difficult for the military to find any clues as to what happened. It was even more important now that several of the Americans had eluded them. He wanted nothing left behind that could be used by the remaining drivers to survive the heat of the ensuing day.

The truck moved slowly on the narrow dirt road as it wound its way through the hills toward Iran. In addition to strict radio silence, a decision had been made weeks earlier to drive without any lights on to avoid the possibility of detection during this part of the journey. Even at this speed they came close to losing their truck several times on sharp curves in the road, stopping just short of plummeting into the canyons below. On occasion they would stop, turning off the engine to listen for any unwanted sounds, like another vehicle on the road behind them or an airplane or helicopter overhead. Nothing, just silence. The farther away they got from the truckers' camp, the safer they felt and the more joyous they became.

The truck had been selected with care. It needed to be small enough to traverse the narrow roads and easy to hide, yet large enough to carry the prisoners. Ali was pleased at the time they saved because it had a full tank of gas.

Once the group had crossed the border into Iran they began a boisterous celebration, some jumping off the truck and dancing in the road. They had long since removed the brush they had tied on back to hide the tire tracks.

The plan had worked almost to perfection. The goal was to capture everyone in the camp and hold them for ransom, along with other demands. The fact that several had escaped and they had to kill one of them lessened the dollar amount they would be able to extort. Of course, it was always desirable to kill an American infidel.

This small group of militants, currently operating out of a tiny village in Iran with the cooperation and assistance of the Iranian Revolutionary Guard, had come a long way from its humble beginnings. And the assistance of their informant within the camp had proven to be invaluable. He told them everything they needed to know about the installation.

Ali had personally chosen the Tiger Trucking Company along with this camp as his target. He had waited a long time for the opportunity. The company had just signed a large contract with the new government of Iraq. Ali and his brethren wanted to make an example of anyone helping the new regime. As far as which camp to hit, the decision had been easy. He laughed at its simplicity. Camp Mojave was located in a remote area with the only help over a hundred miles away. The guards were inexperienced locals, many handling firearms for the first time in their lives. The time had come for his group to exploit the weaknesses of the infidels, and they had done just that.

A rising star in al-Qa'ida (or phonetically and westernized al-Qaeda), Ali Salim had ventured into Iran to obtain an audience with Sahir Umar, a senior operative in the Iranian Revolutionary Guard. Sahir had assisted in the strategic planning of Ali's daring attack, supplying his group with knowledge from his vast experience, as well as food and state-of-the-art weapons. If this group had been dangerous before, they were far more formidable now with this newly formed alliance.

As the truck moved slowly along through the night, Ali secretly gloated over what would ultimately happen. He knew that when word of this glorious moment became public knowledge, the outrage by the Americans would be instantaneous. The Iraqi people would then know that al-Qa'ida was the real force in their country, that they, not the invading American infidels, were the ones in control.

Glorious thoughts of the future raced through his head. This raid would dramatically improve his beloved country of Iraq. He also had visions of how this was going to enhance his own standing in the movement to ultimately rid his country of the infidel intruders, and how it might even help correct conditions in neighboring countries that had been providing support for their cause. In just a matter of days he and his men will have changed the course of history.

Ali was relieved to have succeeded in this daring attack without any of his men being harmed. Allah was on their side. Nothing could stop them now. Nothing!

ℜ

Just past three in the morning, Charlie Johnson's truck sputtered and came to a stop. They were out of gas and they hadn't yet caught up to the terrorists.

"Damn it! I had hoped we'd get farther than this."

"You did good, Charlie," Owens said. "We got a lot farther than I thought we would."

Johnson reached under the seat for his tools, placing them safely in the deep pocket of his jacket. The others climbed out of the truck taking the beef jerky and water with them before pushing the truck off the side of the road into the bushes.

"The fewer who know we're here, the better," Owens said. "Less chance of being dogged by other terrorists. Come on, we walk."

"Couldn't we just sleep in the truck and start out again in the morning?" Numley asked.

"The farther they get, the less chance we'll have of ever finding them. We've got to keep moving."

Owens prodded them along, although they were more tired than they'd ever been in their lives and already thinking about giving up. This was too much to ask of them, especially at their age. But what kept them going was hope. That Numley's truck couldn't go much farther either, and with a little luck it might have already stopped putting everyone on foot. That would make it a lot easier to close the gap between them.

ℜ

Plodding along in the dark, Keith Jacobs lamented his decision to take a job in Iraq in the first place. Financial need was, of course, the now senseless reason he gave himself at the time. He had earned a comfortable living during his life, but like a lot of people, invested almost every penny in the stock market. When it crashed during the early years of the new millennium, it left him with little to show for his efforts.

He still owed on his mortgage, having lost the money that could have paid it off in the market as well. The house could be sold, but neither he nor his wife, Lynn, wanted to do that...at least not yet. Like a lot of people in their late fifties, he had considerable debt and no income to pay it off. Filing for bankruptcy was not an option either; that just wasn't in his character. As for retirement...well, it was out of the question.

Jacobs begrudgingly thought about the two screw jobs he had received in his career that led to this bad situation. The first by a trusted friend who betrayed not only him, but also a partner who financed the new insurance company he had helped to start. If the former friend had paid off as promised when he lured Jacobs to the northwest, Jacobs would have been financially secure for the rest of his life, based on the profitable results he and the senior partner had been able to deliver. Instead, after the company was up and running, the now ex-friend got rid of his partner and took everything Jacobs had built away from him, assigning the responsibilities to newly hired executives. His pride forced him to leave a company he loved along with a friendship that had been destroyed through no fault of his own. That was the last time Jacobs ever fully trusted anyone in the business world.

His last position before taking the job in Iraq was division sales manager for another life insurance company. For several years his division was at the top. But people without industry experience had been brought in to manage the company, and their decisions were destroying the morale of the sales force. He'd attempted to give senior management advice from his previous experience, but they ignored him. As sales plummeted, someone had to take the fall, and Keith Jacobs was terminated. He sought other similar positions, knowing he brought tremendous value to any company that hired him, but he was in his late fifties and the industry was looking for younger sales managers.

So here he was, working in Iraq, perhaps about to do something he never thought possible.

ℜ

Rather than staying on the lengthier winding road, the old guys took several shortcuts over smaller hills in an effort to lessen the gap between them and the terrorists...though not without peril. On several occasions one or another would stumble. Johnson took the worst fall; severely scraping his leg on a rock as he first fell, then rolled partway down a hill they were traversing. He landed hard but handled it well.

By the time the others gathered around him, Johnson was gasping for air and muttering, "Damn it! Now I've gone and done it...swallowed my chaw!" Then he felt his leg. "Aw hell, my leg's wet. It's gotta be blood."

Owens knelt down and asked, "Can you walk on it?"

He got up and put some weight on the leg. "Yep, it still works. Good thing it was my strong leg."

Owens quickly tied a handkerchief around the leg to keep anything else from entering the wound. "We'll fix it up later. Let's go. We'll stay on the road until daylight."

Jacobs and Numley looked at each other and shrugged as Owens walked away. They helped Johnson to his feet and the three of them set off after their leader. They knew they had to pick up the pace…smart enough to know if they lost track of the truck, they too would be lost.

Day Two – Sunday, January 8th

THE BRIGHT RAYS of the sun with its blessed light finally streamed over the Iranian mountaintop after a very long night. Now, at last, they could see. Fortunately it would take several more hours before its ungodly heat would be fully felt. The old guys had traveled all night hoping at every turn to find the truck they were pursuing deserted by the terrorists. Though exhausted, they walked or trotted whenever Owens had the notion. As they continued their trek eastward with its increasingly higher altitude, the night had grown colder, but they'd hardly noticed as their exertion kept them warm.

Other than exhaustion, the greatest sacrifice was the rationing of water. Allowing themselves only small sips to preserve their supply, which did nothing to quench their thirst, they were down to a small amount in the last bottle carried by Owens. Thinking optimistically, they kept the empty bottles to refill along the way. Without any discussion, they all knew it would be nearly impossible to last a full day without more water.

Although there had not been any border check—not on *this* little dirt road—they knew that they had to be in Iran by now. Having already traveled a considerable distance, they were now concerned about how far the terrorists planned to take their prisoners. Iraq was bad enough. Going deeper into

Iran just added to the risk they were taking. Of course if it were too far, it wouldn't matter. They would be unable to save anyone – they would already be dead.

𝕽

The sun had been up for several hours when the truck, filled with prisoners, came to a sudden and unexpected stop. They had made good time, getting closer to where they would hide the infidels and be protected from the outside world. After attempting to start it a few times Ali decided to check the gas tank. He and the driver used a branch from a nearby bush to measure the level. The tip came out wet. They still had fuel. So why had the truck stopped? They opened the hood, pulled a few wires, tapped the carburetor along with the battery cables and then tried to start it again. Nothing. Clearly, the truck wasn't going any farther and none of Ali's men had enough mechanical experience to try and fix it. They had no choice. They had to walk.

Ali commanded, "Get all prisoners out of the truck."

The captives, still bound, were lined up behind the truck and directed to push it off the road with their shoulders.

"Lay some brush against the back to hide it, and sweep away the tire tracks. We don't want it seen by anyone using this road."

Once the truck was completely hidden they tied a long rope to each captive, further minimizing their opportunity to escape. The prisoners were then directed to move forward in a straight line, following each other at arm's length toward their ultimate hiding place.

After a slow and treacherous walk of approximately four miles, the blind prisoners—stumbling and sometimes falling along the way only to be kicked and beaten until they got to their feet—were ordered to stop in front of a clump of bushes at the base of a small hill. The brush was pulled away exposing the entrance to a cave, one just large enough to let a medium-sized truck pass through.

The captives were led into the cave, their footprints erased by branches and the bushes pulled back in front of the entrance. It was as if they had never been there. Ali and his brethren were at last safely concealed within a place that had been well equipped for their arrival.

It had taken over two months to prepare the cave for this moment. Its original use was for Saddam Hussein as a temporary hiding place if in fact the Americans and their allies did attack Iraq and were able to defeat his troops. It was not uncommon for dignitaries to hide from their enemies in caves and even spider holes until it was safe to move to a better location. This cave had been equipped with an electrical generator for lighting and other amenities.

Saddam had selected Iran rather than one of the other neighboring countries, figuring that his enemies would consider it the least likely place he would go. He did not think there would be an attack on Baghdad because ten years earlier the United States had thousands of soldiers and equipment on Iraq's southern border defending Kuwait, but never ventured toward his city. A million-man army was intimidating; therefore he was confident that the rhetoric being communicated to him through the United Nations dignitaries and U.S. Secretary of State was just sword-rattling in an attempt to make him bow down and relinquish rights he so enjoyed as the president of Iraq. This would never happen while he was the Sovereign Ruler of his country. However, in preparation for the unlikely event his enemies prevailed, he had utilized the services of a trusted Iraqi al-Qa'ida operative, Ali Salim, to find a suitable hiding place for him across the border.

Once the cave had been found and made ready, Hussein gave Ali two crates. One was tightly sealed, the other open and empty. The instructions were to immediately place the sealed crate in the cave, telling no one about it. The second crate was to be kept by Ali, and at the first sign of an attack on the capitol city itself, he was to break into the National Museum in Baghdad with some of his men and take specific items. He was directed to wrap the items carefully, place them in the open crate and seal it in a similar manner as the first one. This crate would then be transported in the bed of a small supply truck to the hidden cave where the two of them were to remain closed until Saddam's arrival. To ensure this, he had his initials SdH and the Iraqi Royal Seal emblazoned in red and black on each crate along with the words, *Do Not Touch*. Ali, of course, had no idea what was inside the first crate. Hussein had merely referred to the contents as his personal effects. They were still closed, even though Saddam was now in custody, because no Muslim follower in his right mind—whether Iraqi or Iranian—would countermand a directive of Saddam Hussein and expect to live. He had too many dedicated followers.

It was only after Hussein's capture in the now infamous spider hole that had taken place a dozen days before Christmas in 2003, just a handful of months after the attack on Baghdad, that Ali decided to use the cave for another purpose, one that would honor the name of their fallen ruler and be detrimental to the American infidels. At the time he made that decision, of course, he didn't know what that purpose would be.

The cave was well equipped and ready for their arrival. Cages for cells had been installed the previous week to make it even more difficult for the prisoners to escape. Mats were available for Ali's men, and would be used for eating, sleeping and praying. In addition there was a refrigerator, video camcorder and television set, all run by the gasoline driven electrical generator. The television was connected to a small satellite dish well hidden in a tree outside the cave. Supplies were to be delivered daily from the Iranian village where Ali and his men had trained, a four-hour drive each way, with the driver also acting as courier to relay information to and from the village.

The first order of business: videotape the masked leader dictating the demands of his group to the world. In preparation for this event and its impact on the dignitaries and masses that would be seeing it, the prisoners were forced to kneel in a group behind Ali as he faced the camera. It was only then that the rope attached to each captured driver was removed. Ali's men, all of whom had put their hooded masks back on, took their positions at each end of the group with two stationed in the center behind them. The camcorder was turned on and positioned first for a wide-angle shot of the group, then a close-up of Ali.

More than ready to deliver his speech, Ali paused a moment for effect and then read his prepared remarks in English.

"Behind me you see the American infidels who have been spying on our beloved country of Iraq disguised as truck drivers. One even pretends to be a consultant for the trucking company. This is unacceptable and all must pay dearly for this deception. Our demands are as follows: pull out all American troops from Iraq and immediately release the prisoners you are holding in Abu Ghraib. They are all innocent. If the American government refuses these demands, Tiger Trucking Company has one other choice. You will pay us one million dollars for each man you want released. If you want them all, you will pay us a total of thirteen million dollars. Knowing you will need time to obtain the money, we will give you until next Friday, the thirteenth of your month, to comply with our demands. Failing to do so will result in the execution of the first infidel, with another executed each day until the full amount of money is received or all of your men are dead. The choice is yours. Give us your answer by announcing it on the national Baghdad television station. You will be contacted for a drop off site. Remember, their lives are in your hands."

The camera went to black and the taping was over. Every demand included a pullout of American troops, but Ali already knew the reality of that request, and that it wouldn't happen anytime soon. The president of the United States had made it clear to everyone, even dissenters in his own country, that he wasn't going to provide any timetable or finite date for the withdrawal of the troops. The rationale was valid when it came to this enemy. The Muslim followers, if nothing else, were patient. Their cause had existed for centuries. If a firm date were known in advance, they would just wait, even if it meant a decade or more. The United States would not give them that leverage.

Just prior to the taping, a small truck loaded with food and other supplies had arrived. Ali handed the tape to the driver. His job was to hand it off to a confidant for delivery to the television networks—not only to the Al-Jaazera Network in the Middle East, but CNN and the Fox News Network as well. It was anticipated that all stations would air it worldwide. No doubt this would be big news.

With the camera now off, the masked men let out a shout and congratulated Ali for such a fine speech. The prisoners were then prodded to their feet and herded into a giant cage strategically located at the back of the cave, the farthest point from its entrance. The duct tape was removed from the eyes of the last prisoner as he was being pushed in—Butch Simkins.

As he removed the tape the captor whispered under his breath so no one else would hear, "You can release the rest of your filthy pig friends here, but do it without making a sound. Not one sound!"

After the door to the cage had been securely fastened with a large padlock, the captors all sat down with food and drink facing the cage to observe a potentially humorous situation—American prisoners attempting to determine if it would be safe to untie themselves—and if so, how to do it.

"Now we can watch these infidels demonstrate their stupidity. It could take them hours to get the tape off."

Simkins was the only one who could see, but still couldn't do much with hands that were securely fastened behind his back, and tape over his mouth. The other prisoners had no idea he could free them, and in fact had been directed to do so—but without making a sound.

"No talking. That means you." Ali sat down with his men, directing his comment at Simkins, coupled with a steely glare that only Simkins could see.

The directive puzzled Simkins. He didn't want to do anything that would cause *more* trouble. He cautiously bumped one of the truckers and got bumped back with a low grumble that sounded like *watch it* from behind the tape for his effort. The onlookers snickered. This was just what they had anticipated from these foolish infidels. He bumped into another one with similar results. With each rejection the laughter grew louder. Simkins looked over at his captors trying to understand what was so funny, but couldn't figure it out. They laughed again and began to verbally ridicule the captives...in Arabic of course. None of the captives realized that they were the reason for the laughter—they were the show.

In frustration Simkins bumped Richard Murdock. The consultant, already suspecting something was going on, lightly bumped him back. Butch did it again and received another bump. They were silently communicating with each other much to the disdain of the captors, whose laughter immediately stopped.

Butch inched around Murdock so that their backs and hands were touching. He then searched for the end of the tape and unwound it from around his wrists. Once his hands were free, Murdock removed the tape from his eyes and then his mouth, and immediately knew what to do next. He took the tape off Butch's mouth and from around his wrists. The two of them then started the job of freeing the others.

After the tape had been removed from the prisoners, it was at once obvious that if they ever hoped to escape, they would have to go through all of their captors, now located between them and the cave's exit. Not likely. As this fact set in, morale dropped even lower, which was exactly what Ali and his men wanted. The plan from the very beginning was to humiliate and punish these prisoners until they had lost all hope of surviving. Mental anguish with total dominance was always part of the torment.

Ali glared at his captives, savoring their looks of despair. He spat loudly into the cage, "You filthy infidels. This is where you will be cleansed of your former ways. It will be your own personal purgatory of pain."

The informant leaned over and whispered in his ear, "The big one over there, the one with the short blond hair is mine." He pointed at Simkins. "I will take great pleasure in breaking him into tiny little pieces."

Ali laughed and said, "He's all yours. We have both waited a long time for this and now it is your turn to be rewarded for your patience."

ℜ

Ali's followers prepared for sleep, even though it was early in the day. They were tired from the attack, and the long trek from the trucker's camp. The beatings would begin the following day.

There was great pleasure in seeing the flesh of an American infidel burst open when pummeled by a gloved fist, or hear a bone break when struck just right with one of the metal bars they had stocked in the cave. Great joy was also felt when a prisoner groaned and begged for mercy with cries to stop. But best of all was watching blood splatter on the dirt, seeing the horrified look of the beaten man, knowing that it was *his* blood seeping into the earth.

Ali would vent his anger at the Americans by personally conducting a majority of the beatings, although he would let his men participate in many as well. After learning about some of the drivers from his informant, he already detested them, in addition to his disdain for Americans and their decadent ways in general. In his mind, all American infidels lived in a sinful society. He had read their newspapers and viewed their newscasts. He saw what happened in America on a daily basis. During his lifetime he had also seen many of their movies and television shows and knew how they lived and interacted with one another. Everyone in America had money, a lot of it. They spent it on big houses, sometimes more than one, and many large and pretentious foreign automobiles—another sign of their arrogance. And their women paraded around on their streets in skimpy clothing revealing their bodies to anyone passing by. Whores! As he often said to his followers, "The lack of proper clothing on women is the beginning of their debauchery." He was not about to tolerate that type of lifestyle and behavior in his country, if he had anything to say about it.

Most of the men were lax about keeping their masks on when in view of the prisoners. They weren't the most comfortable things to wear for long periods of time. Besides, to most Americans they knew that they all looked the same. Ali noticed with interest, however, that his informant kept his mask on at all times after having changed out of the clothing he had been wearing so the prisoners would not recognize him. He also made sure they did not hear him speak. He didn't want them identifying his voice. If the prisoners were actually released—debatable at this time whether the demands were met or not—he wanted to be able to return to a similar job and again help his brethren from the inside in the planning of future attacks.

The informant, of all Ali's people, was most loyal to the cause. They shared a common bond—they were cousins.

They also shared a common tragedy. His wife and son had been killed along with Ali's family in the early stages of the American attack on Baghdad. They had been visiting Ali's family whose home was in the same neighborhood as a cousin of Saddam Hussein that had been bombed the very first night, the result of a tip that Saddam would be there. The American forces thought they had been successful, but heard later that they had just missed him and his two sons. During the bombing, Ali's home was hit and both families instantly killed. Neither would ever forget nor forgive the American intruders. Ali and the informant had been in the countryside when the bombing took place, or they too would have been killed. Instead, they discovered their families' mangled bodies in the rubble when they returned the following morning. Nearby neighbors confirmed it had been bombs from U.S. warplanes that had been responsible. As neither now had a family to care for, they focused their entire being on revenge. The two of them vowed then and there that they would get even—no matter how long it took.

What neither of them could know was that the home had been hit, not by an American bomb, but by a guided missile from one of Saddam Hussein's own defending artillery positions attempting to protect their city. It completely missed its target in the sky, and plummeted back to earth, striking Ali's home.

The U.S. Air Force used smart bomb technology during this raid, just as they had in Afghanistan, the latest version produced by Boeing. Instead of a video camera or laser seeker to steer the bomb toward its target, it used a GPS satellite signal that is effective in good weather and bad. The bomb doesn't have to see its target to hit it. When dropped from a plane, a control system and adjustable fins give the bomb the ability to steer itself as it glides through the air. When everything works correctly, these bombs generally hit within a few feet of their targets.

Ali and the informant would never know this highly important nuance about what really happened that fateful night. As a result, their rage was channeled in the wrong direction, but would never change. They had said many times during the planning phase of the attack that the Americans would pay dearly for what they did to their families. It would be their personal jihad for as long as they lived.

And now, they would be able to take out some of this pent-up anger on these captured truck drivers. Tomorrow couldn't come soon enough.

ℜ

Having walked over half the night and most of the day sustained by beef jerky and a few sips of water, the old guys couldn't go any farther. Although there had been no sign of the truck with its prisoners, they had to stop and regroup. At the moment it was more important to rest and then find water or they would never make it through another day. If it had not been for the physical training Owens had started conducting shortly after he arrived at Camp Mojave, they wouldn't have made it this far. The last twenty hours confirmed that those exercises had helped all of them immensely.

They left the road, finding an area protected by foliage and rocks, collapsing on the ground exhausted. Not a word was said as they fell into a deep sleep.

Owens awakened first, and as there was still some daylight left, he roused the others to take advantage of it. Each went through a myriad of complaints about why they shouldn't be getting up just yet.

Owens asked, "How's that leg doing Charlie?"

"It hurts like hell."

"We better take a look, make sure there's no infection setting in."

They gently pulled the handkerchief away from the wound. "It might hurt, but it looks pretty good, although it's too early to tell for sure."

"Well that's a relief."

"Keep the rag off so it can get some air," Owens ordered. "It'll heal up faster too. OK?"

"Yep! Good idea, and I'll keep it elevated on this rock while we're here. Shouldn't we wash it off?"

Numley, in utter amazement asked, "With what? We're almost out of water. The bigger question is how to find more way out here. And how do we get our hands on some food? I'm thinking we should have stayed at the camp and waited for help."

"You could have stayed, Rodney. No one forced you to come."

Jabaar, who surprisingly was still with them said, "You ask about water. Finding it will be very difficult. Almost impossible. Only hope is to search for place, then dig."

Jacobs asked, "Where do we start and what do we have to do?"

"We very fortunate. Travels take us east. We now closer to mountains. Lots of water in underground streams. It goes downhill. We must find old riverbed, the lowest spot. Then make scraping tools from trees. Dig. Very difficult, but it can be done—follow me."

They set off after him. An hour later Jabaar stopped and said, "We try here."

The area was farther away from the road than their campsite and down in a small ravine. Jabaar had noticed it earlier, but had hoped to find an even better location. They quickly set to work. Branches were broken off trees and made into crude shovels. Everyone started to dig. By this time they could hardly move. But the young guard knew he couldn't do it alone, and so did Owens, so he prodded them on. "Come on guys. If you want to survive, you've got to give more than you ever thought possible."

Jabaar added, "If religious, pray to your God for strength and success. Guidance from higher being is good."

As they dug, Rodney asked Jabaar, "You talk about praying, but that's the reason we're in this mess in the first place. Why do Muslims hate Christians so much?"

"Not all Muslims hate Christians. There are different types of Muslims. Many don't even like each other. Three main groups are Sunni, Shi'ites, Kurds. All follow rule of Islam started in seventh century by Muhammad. Christians also in Iraq, but very small, maybe only million."

"Then you have freedom of religion? Not that it matters to me because I don't even believe in God."

"No. Radical Muslims say two religions cannot coexist peacefully, but that not every Muslim. Jesus mentioned many times in Qur'an, the book of Islam."

Keith Jacobs exclaimed, "Jesus in the Koran? I didn't know that."

"My family is Folk Islam, not Orthodox. Much more tolerant. Muslims who become Christians believe words in both Qur'an and Bible. Muhammad say writers corrupted Bible, that it is untruthful and inferior to Qur'an."

"Is that the biggest difference between the two religions then, a corrupted Bible?"

"Islam emphatic that it be only religion. Go to paradise? Must be Muslim following rule of Islam—completely. Anything else, you go to hell instead. Allah is the only God, and most important part of Islam. He is same God as Christians. Difference, Christians pray through Jesus; Muslims not need Jesus for prayer to Allah."

"Then what's this jihad stuff all about?"

"Most people think jihad only mean holy war and death to infidels. It is much more. It is a commitment to spread and defend Islam in many ways. Jihad of Tongue *speaks* about faith. Jihad of Hand means faith in good works. Jihad of

Heart makes faith a force for good. Then there is Jihad of Sword—defend faith when under attack."

Numley pressed, "So violence is part of the religion, then!"

"It became aggressive after existing several hundred years in eleventh century when Christians start the Crusades. Both religions have blood on hands."

Jacobs shrugged. "You said the Koran talks about Jesus. Why would He be mentioned at all?"

"Because He is great Prophet, like Adam, Noah, Abraham, Moses and Muhammad. The Qur'an says Jesus is Son of Mary by virgin birth. Followers are Christians. On judgment day, He will play a role along with Muhammad. Qur'an also said He was taken into Heaven, but is silent on resurrection from tomb."

"What does silent mean?"

"It says Jesus do many miracles, but He was not crucified, dead, buried, or go to heaven by resurrection. Islam does not believe in Trinity of God the Father, Son, Holy Ghost. Muslims believe in only one God, Allah. It is blasphemous to believe otherwise."

"Wow. How can a former Muslim, with this strict teaching, ever believe in anything else?"

"They see no conflict. Allah is all-powerful. Can take any form He chooses, like man on earth in form of Jesus or even a risen being. He is still one God, Allah. The resurrected Jesus showed himself and wounds from crucifixion to disciples and many other people after rock rolled away from tomb and it was empty. That was a miracle. Rock impossible to move once it seal opening. Resurrection is believable because so many saw Him before He rose to heaven. Believers are considered infidels."

"What's all this about the Bible being corrupted?"

"I don't believe it. Disciples, each one writing separately, documented His life. Matthew even made notes during life of Jesus. Muhammad's followers wrote Qur'an twenty years after His death. No mention of notes direct from Muhammad. Again, I believe teachings of Qur'an, also what Bible says. Both in purest form teach peace—"

"Water! Water's filling up the hole!" Numley was the first to see the water as they had continued to dig during Jabaar's discussion on religion. Their success was only realized after another grueling hour of scraping. It started with a trickle that formed a small pool at the bottom of the hole.

All were instantly elated about this accomplishment. They had discovered water out in the desert of a strange and foreign land, experiencing their first real success in this impossible journey. They were also relieved because they knew that with water, they would be able to survive another day.

ℜ

Richard Murdock observed the other prisoners, all prone and deep in thought with fears about what lie ahead. Shaking uncontrollably, each experienced their own violent nightmare of what would be happening to them during the next few days, maybe starting in the next few minutes for all they knew. Increased blood pressure and shortness of breath surely amplified the anxiety taking control of their bodies. They doubted that they would survive. This was the end. The only question was when. How would anyone find them in time? Tears flowed freely down some faces. A few closed their eyes tightly, but were unable to abate their tears. They wondered why they had come to Iraq in the first place and wished they hadn't. All they had wanted to do was earn a lot of money transporting needed food and supplies throughout this war-racked country. Now, in hindsight, it hadn't been worth it.

Murdock had been traveling incognito, for his own personal preservation. If it had been known how wealthy he was, he would have been a primary target for every terrorist and insurgent in the country. It was well known by the terrorists that negotiating with the representatives of one man for his freedom was less difficult than dealing with a country or even a corporation. And it was much easier for Murdock to move around if everyone thought he was just a consultant looking for ways to help the companies he was supposed to be representing cut costs to increase their profits. Yet in spite of all the secrecy, here he was, a prisoner anyway, with his life on the line.

Captured with a group of young and inexperienced men, he knew they had not yet been around long enough to be tested in life. For most of them, coming to Iraq was the first time they had left their zip code. While not quite twice their age, he had endured many more things along the way...though of course, nothing like this. He knew, however, that this group of men would need his help and guidance, and even then they still might crumble. He too was scared, but he also knew that everyone in this cage had to stay as calm as possible if they had any hope of surviving the torture they would doubtless endure.

Before leaving for Iraq, Murdock had read about handling pain without medication. Although not yet fifty, he was already experiencing the effects of arthritis in parts of his body and hated the thought of taking pain pills the rest of his life. He had heard about controlling pain with relaxation techniques and distraction strategies, and he'd already started practicing these methods on himself. He knew they worked; and was a believer.

After it appeared that all the terrorists had fallen asleep, Murdock quietly told everyone to move their heads toward the center of the cage so he could communicate with them without being detected. If his whispering was heard, the terrorists would not know who was talking, which would prevent him from being singled out and punished even more severely than the others.

"Listen up everyone. I've got some ideas that might help you get through this nightmare a little easier."

"A magic genie?" Simpkins said. "She blinks her eyes and we're out of here?"

"Not quite that good, Butch, but something that can help. Do you want to know what I'm talking about or just be a wise ass?"

"We're listening," was the reply from several of the others.

"I think all of us know that these terrorists are going to make us suffer. You can see it in their eyes." He sensed a shudder go through the men as he said the words everyone was afraid to admit.

"It will take the intelligence capabilities of our military to find us and get us out of here, and even then, some of us will probably be killed. But, nobody else can possibly help us right now, so we have to survive on our own. We will be tortured. You can bank on it. Their hatred for us is undeniable. But maybe some things I've learned can help make it a little more tolerable."

Murdock then described what he had practiced about minimizing pain without medication. He told them they would need to be their own support group, assuring each other that it was OK to give in when the individual's tolerance for pain had been reached, which would be different for each person.

"Eventually they'll extract what they want from us, like admitting we're spies against their country, or sign a document like they have with other hostages. Each one of us will ultimately succumb or die in the process."

He went on to say that everyone needed to hold out as long as possible, but without antagonizing their captors in the process. They should try to convince them that they were telling the truth.

"But in the end, everyone in here will do whatever they want us to do once we have passed our personal limits."

"How will we know?" Lewis asked.

A couple of the men gave a half-hearted laugh and one whispered, "You'll know."

Murdock waited a few moments, just in case any of the terrorists had overheard them, and then explained the process of controlling pain, emphasizing the need for total concentration under extreme stress. They would have to focus on other things. And it would need to start while still in the cage watching a buddy being tortured.

"Take slow deep breaths. This floods your central nervous system with oxygen and other chemicals that will help improve your comfort."

Progressive relaxation that can also reduce pain was described, but he added that it was extremely difficult to do. The goal with this method was to relax every muscle beginning with the toes, working up to the head.

"When you breathe in, tense your muscles. Hold your breath for a few seconds and then when you breathe out, let your body go limp. Use your imagination to think about something peaceful, a deliberate daydream about a nice experience. The more detailed the better. The mind becomes absorbed doing this rather than focusing on the pain."

"It won't be easy, but if it decreases the pain, even just a little, the torture will be more endurable. Let's get some sleep while they're leaving us alone. It might be our *only* rest."

They fell quiet, except for an occasional sob from one of the horribly frightened drivers.

𝕽

Butch Simkins, now terrified, had crawled over to the farthest corner of the cage to cry as quietly as possible without being detected. He didn't feel tough anymore; he couldn't even pretend. His mind flashed back to what had brought him to Iraq in the first place.

All of his life Simkins had practiced what he called *going with the moment,* doing whatever he wanted, when he wanted. It occasionally got him in trouble at work, but never with the authorities until one night, while driving around, he crashed a party at a private home in an upscale neighborhood. As he was a novelty to the middle-aged partygoers, they invited him to stay and share their cocaine. This was his first time to snort coke and it hit him hard. Combined with all the alcohol he had already consumed, he managed to pass out in a back bedroom. The small but well-proportioned blond woman he had coaxed back there got bored with her new young stud, so she put her clothes back on and went out to find someone else to party with, leaving him sound asleep in the dark.

In the early morning hours, he was suddenly awakened by what sounded like a gunshot. He heard a woman screaming and then another shot was fired. He was fully awake in seconds, and scared. Quietly he crept to the door, putting an ear against it in an effort to hear what was being said. A girl's voice could be heard crying and begging for mercy, asking someone to please put the gun down before somebody got hurt. She was arguing that she didn't mean any harm, that it was just innocent fun. She promised never to do it again.

The other person, obviously drunk, slurred his words as he told her, "It's too late you dumb little bitch, you've already done it and you've ruined my career. I'm screwed for the rest of my life."

Then there was a third shot and a moment later the sound of a door being slammed. After that…silence.

Simkins listened intently for several more minutes before determining the house was empty. Although still groggy from the booze and cocaine, he put on his clothes and tiptoed down the hall. As he entered the party room with its empty glasses and food platters strewn throughout, he immediately saw a half naked woman lying on the floor, her chest covered with blood. A stainless steel pistol lay on the floor beside her. He reached over the dead girls body and picked it up—it was still warm. While leaning over the girl, he looked at her face and remembered that she was the one he had taken to the bedroom earlier that evening. He thought they'd had sex, but couldn't remember for sure. If they did, he had seen enough on television to know that the DNA evidence could be incriminating. He further wondered if that was the reason she had been shot, because she had screwed around with him. He shuddered at the thought that the guy who killed her might come after him. This was more terrifying than the police, but both were enough to make him run, and as quickly as possible.

Simkins decided that, since no one else was around, and because he had crashed the party, nobody knew his full name. The house was even in another city. He had told them his name was Butch, but they were so stoned, they started calling him Buddy. He didn't care what they called him as long as he had a good time with their dope and their women.

He put the warm pistol in his pocket, and smiling smugly, he used a cocktail napkin to open and close the front door. He knew all about fingerprints too. He quickly walked to his car, but was smart enough not to run and draw attention to himself at this hour. Quietly opening his car door, he got in behind the wheel and drove off into what was left of the night.

Two days later there was an announcement on television that the body of a woman had been discovered. The police said that their Crime Scene Investigation unit was going over every detail, and described the type of gun that had killed her. They said it appeared she had been attending a party and had participated in sexual intercourse, and that they were in the process of analyzing a DNA sample of the man in addition to the numerous fingerprints they had found throughout the house. They advised the perpetrator to turn himself in before they caught him, that the proceedings would go much easier.

Although Simkins had tried to cover his tracks, he had forgotten to wipe his prints off the bedroom door. He was petrified with fear. As the last person to leave that bedroom, his prints would be on top of anyone else who might also have been in there. He figured he was a dead man if they connected him to the party and the murdered girl. No one would believe he hadn't killed her. For the first time he realized he had to leave the country, and fast, but to do it without making anyone suspicious. The question was how?

That afternoon his friends, Bud Tompkins and Leslie Lewis, stopped by and told him about a truck-driving job in Iraq. The pay was awesome and they could start right away. In his mind it was the perfect cover to leave town on short notice. The three of them interviewed with a representative from the trucking company the next day and all were hired. Simkins, his friends and the newfound gun left for Baghdad that following weekend on a corporate jet along with other newly hired drivers. As the wheels left the ground and the mid-sized jet rocketed skyward, Simkins smiled inside realizing it couldn't have been a more perfect escape.

Now, as he lay shivering in a corner of the cage, he suddenly realized what a fool he had been. His only hope now was for a second chance.

ℜ

The old guys may have avoided being captured, but at a great physical price. They had climbed over rocks, fallen down hills and walked all night and much of the day. After a brief sleep, they had searched for water and dug for hours to get it. And their only food since dinner last night had been a few small pieces of beef jerky.

Jabaar told them of the time he and his father had camped out, and how wild animals had visited a nearby pool of water during the night, as it was safer for them to drink after dark. He reminded them that an animal's sense of smell was far greater than that of a human, that an animal might smell the new supply of water and come to investigate.

Owens suggested a plan. "We need more rest before starting out again. The best thing we can do now is to move downwind from the pool and take turns standing watch. We can use one of these sticks as a spear if an animal shows up to drink some water."

The group was indeed fortunate that Jabaar had stayed with them. They had used his knife to cut the branches and whittle them into makeshift shovels, and now a spear. And while he did have a rifle, any plan for gathering food excluded the use of a gun. They couldn't afford to fire it for fear of being heard. They hadn't seen anyone, but still had to be cautious.

Jacobs took the first watch. The others settled into a deep sleep a hundred yards away. After the sun had set it grew bitterly cold in the ravine. Fortunately they had taken their jackets with them. Little did they know they would be sleeping on the dirt miles away, using these same jackets as protection from the elements the very next night.

It was still pitch dark, and would remain that way for a couple more nights before the moon could help out. The sense of sound was about the only way to guard the others from danger. Jacobs listened to the sounds of the night more intently than at any other time he could remember. He knew that his life, as well as the others, depended upon it.

Just yesterday he had grudgingly bemoaned his decision to work in Iraq and live in a trucker camp. Now he didn't even have that. He was outdoors trying to find terrorists, and even worse, he was supposed to help save other men, and several of them had been assholes to him and the others stuck out here with him.

He kept thinking about how unrealistic this set of circumstances was. They didn't yet know where the terrorists were, only that they had gone in this direction. They didn't have a plan once they found them, if they did; and they only had one gun. They were going to get themselves killed. Lynn was right—again. He should have listened to her. They didn't need the money that bad, but no, he had to be greedy. This was not good, not good at all. He sat there in the dark, shaking his head and thinking about how bad things were. He knew he was in a dangerous situation and all he could do was lament the fact that a few short months earlier he had made the worst decision of his life.

After two hours, Jacobs crept over to the others and woke up Numley so that he could take the next watch. He handed him the rustic wooden spear with the whittled point and wished him luck in bagging a wild animal in the dark, if one showed up.

Numley, like Jacobs, couldn't believe his circumstances. He wasn't a fighter. He'd never owned a gun and had never even gone hunting with his buddies who condoned the barbaric sport. He had never killed anything in his life except an occasional bug. Now, he was expected to not only spot a wild animal in the dark, but also kill it so that they would have something to eat. He started silently singing the words of a song from one of his favorite musicals.

To dream, the impossible dream…

After about an hour, Numley thought he heard something from the direction of the water hole. First, the sound was faint, but then it grew louder. Yes, it was the sound of water being lapped up, the same sound his dog used to make when drinking water from his bowl in the kitchen. He had to get closer without being seen or heard…or smelled.

The lookout station had been set up downwind from the water. The greater trick was to *not* be heard by the animal while getting close enough to strike. He slowly and quietly snuck closer to the water hole, and although he could barely see it in the dark, there it was—a scrawny wild dog that looked like a coyote drinking the newly discovered water. The animal was so preoccupied with this newfound treasure that it didn't notice the hunter's advance.

Numley's thoughts raced. He'd never done anything like this before. But hunger won out.

As silently as possible, he leaped through the air with the point of the spear aimed directly at the creature, striking it squarely in the side. The wounded animal screamed in pain then growled as it turned its head towards Numley and snapped its jaws. It then tried to slink into the bushes, but its hind legs wouldn't move.

Jabaar was the first to appear. He grabbed the flailing animal by its ears and stabbed it in the chest. As the creature went limp, he cut its throat and guided its fall to the ground where it lay motionless—bleeding out after having received an *acceptable slaughter*.

In the Iraqi culture—in fact the entire Muslim world—it is important how an animal is killed for food. In the book of Islam, Allah tells followers what they may and may not eat, and further how animals must be slaughtered for its meat to be *halal* or lawful. Halal meat must first be permissible to eat, have some life left in it, and not be contaminated. It must be slaughtered by a Muslim of sound mind, or a follower of the Book (Christian or Jew) who believes in his own book and adheres to its tenets. The actual slaughter is the proper slitting of the throat that was observed by Jabaar when he killed the wild dog. In addition, the name of Allah must be recited before actually cutting the animal's throat. When this full procedure takes place, the animal has been killed in due form, which makes it halal. If not halal, it is *haram*, or prohibited, and cannot be eaten by a Muslim unless driven by necessity. A dog, domesticated donkey, frog and the pig are examples of forbidden meat. In this situation, the wild dog would be forbidden, even though it was slaughtered in due form. However, by necessity, death due to starvation would take precedence over the fact that it was forbidden meat.

Jabaar and Numley stared at the fallen animal in silence. He had done it. Numley had won the first meal for this small group of starving survivors. For the first time in many years, he felt good about himself—really good. And the fact that he had to kill something to feel that way didn't diminish the euphoric feeling. The others quickly joined them, slapping him on the back, congratulating him on the kill—another positive accomplishment for this group of downtrodden men. Johnson was the most excited, knowing a meal was at hand. He, of course, had been reminding everyone it was his beef jerky that had kept them alive up to this point.

Killing an animal in the wilds, of course, was just the first step. Now, they had to cook it without being observed. The safest time to build a fire was while it was dark so the smoke wouldn't be seen rising into the sky. The fire itself would have to be in a pit so its flames would be out of sight, in case someone was traveling on the road at that hour. They started digging again, this time to eat. They found a good location where the dirt was softer than it had been at the water hole, taking only a few minutes to prepare the area for a fire. While two of them took turns digging the pit, the others picked up dead branches and kindling. In the still dark hours of early morning, the fire cooked the wild dog, which had been gutted and skinned by Jabaar in preparation for their first real meal on this desperate journey.

No one admitted to having ever eaten dog meat before. However, the Iraqi guard seemed to know his way around the animal in a way that indicated this wasn't the first time he had done this sort of thing—maybe not with a dog, but definitely with a recently slaughtered animal. Did it taste good? No! But it was better than nothing at all. Everyone agreed they would never again bitch about a poorly cooked meal.

After eating, they decided it would be all right to sleep without anyone on watch for a while as they were all still tired and needed their rest before continuing their search at daybreak. If it had been light enough, they would have all seen the smile on the face of a now contented Charlie Johnson.

Day Three – Monday, January 9th

OWENS AWOKE with a start. Hundreds of concerns raced through his mind. He was the reason they were there. He had been the one to drag them into this dismal situation.

The night had been cold and miserable. They joked about it being a three-dog night for warmth, realizing they had killed and eaten the only dog around. They were thankful for daybreak and the warmth it would provide once they climbed out of the ravine.

Their only plan was to continue along the dirt road in hopes of finding the others before it was too late. Before leaving their camp, they drank as much water as they could and then filled the empty bottles. They wrapped what was left of the dog meat in leaves and assigned Charlie Johnson the job of carrying it, with a warning not to eat any of it along the way. He assured them the vittles would be safe with him.

They climbed back up to the road and resumed their trek. After an hour of walking, Johnson said, "Guys, wait, I've got to take a dump."

He handed the food to Numley and disappeared into the bushes for several minutes. Returning, he shook his head. "That was the worst crapper ever. Not even a corn cob for toilet paper."

A grin spread across his face—often the forerunner of one of his many jokes. "By the way, does anyone know how many men it takes to change a roll of toilet paper?" There was a moment of silence before he continued: "Nobody knows...it's never been done!" Then he laughed his bellowing laugh. "I always liked that one." They continued on their way.

About midmorning Owens gestured for them to stop. "Guys. Tire tracks."

Numley said, "And not just any tracks. It looks like one is almost bald on the left side. This is *my* truck."

"Maybe some of that luck we needed just arrived. The only bad part is, the damn thing is still running. How much gas was left in there, Rodney?"

"I could have sworn there was less than a quarter of a tank. There must've been more than I thought."

"Let's keep going. It can't run *much* longer—I hope."

They continued on down the road following the newly found tracks, walking, even jogging, now energized by their discovery, but still weary from all that had already happened to them.

"Remind me again why we're going to all this trouble?" Johnson asked.

The old guys had been the butt of many of the other drivers' jokes during the early days on the job, and it seemed ironic they were risking their lives to try and save them. Johnson had always thought that Simkins, Lewis, and Tompkins had stayed awake at night coming up with new pranks. And everything they did was simple-minded and immature. Grammar school-type jokes by grown men.

He recalled one bad experience a week after his arrival. The younger drivers, who never tried to deter Butch Simkins from any of his bullshit, could hardly wait for Johnson to sit down to dinner. As he did, a loud noise erupted that shocked everyone not expecting it. A whoopee cushion had been hidden under the cloth pad on the chair. It sounded more like a horse passing gas than a human being. Johnson fell to the floor. Everyone in Iraq was sensitive to loud noises; you never knew when a terrorist was going to set off another bomb. He sprained his wrist in the fall, not to mention his pride. The room broke out into laughter. The old guys helped Johnson to his feet as they glared at the younger men. Simkins and his two cronies raised their beer cans in a condescending salute. The evening's humor at the expense of the older drivers was over. They quickly went back to devouring the evening meal with atrocious table manners and returned to their discussion about large breasted women—or as they referred to them, big-titted bitches.

Johnson shrugged and repeated, "So why are we trying to save these guys again?"

ℜ

The terrorists awakened early, likely eager to start inflicting pain on the captured Americans. Murdock watched them eat a brief breakfast; the prisoners were given water and a small piece of bread. Afterward, two of the largest and meanest looking of them approached the cage, unlocked the door and pulled Leslie Lewis out. He whimpered in fear.

Although the militants had entered the cage more than once since their arrival, their departure always included a dramatic, seemingly symbolic locking of the large padlock. This time, however, the captors seemed so intent on dragging Lewis to the beating post in the center of camp that they forgot to re-lock the cage. This oversight had not gone unnoticed by Bud Tompkins.

Tompkins looked at the others in the cage and then at the terrorists who had gathered around Lewis for the day's first beating. Murdock could tell by Tompkins' expression that he was going to try to escape. He shook his head frantically in an attempt to warn him off. He mouthed the words, *It's a trap. Don't go,* and grabbed his shirtsleeve in an effort to stop him.

Tompkins pulled free, ignoring the warning, and silently opened the door a bit wider and slid out. Crouching as low as possible, he scurried for the cover of the first rock between the cage and his exit to freedom. Murdock held his breath as he watched him skirt around the backs of the terrorists, hoping no one would turn around. Halfway to the rock—almost on cue—the entire group spun around, their rifles pointed directly at him. Tompkins raised his hands in the air and froze. The militant stationed on the other side of the rock came up behind him and drove him into the ground with a slashing blow from his rifle. The terrorists roared their approval. The first blood had been drawn.

They locked the cage and dragged the unconscious Tompkins in front of the other prisoners, stripping him naked and tying his hands behind his back. He was quickly revived with a splash of water.

"You American infidels are stupid," Ali said. "Do you think we would forget to lock your cage?

He pulled Tompkins up on his knees. "Because you must be a leader of these men, demonstrating your prowess for escape..." the group laughed again, "...we will make an example of you."

Murdock watched as one of the minions handed a knife to Ali, the long blade glistening from the lights overhead. The camcorder was turned on and Ali faced it as he held Tompkins up by his hair. "Look closely. This man tried to escape after we warned them not to. He will be the first to die."

Tompkins shouted, "No! Do anything, but please don't kill me. I'll never do it again. I promise!"

"Your promise came too late."

Ali placed the knife against his throat and dragged it back and forth until all he was holding was his head. The body slumped to the ground in a pool of blood. The dismembered head, held aloft, was shown to the camera. Then Ali turned to Murdock and the drivers and rolled it toward their cage like a bowling ball. They gasped in horror. Several vomited.

"If anyone else tries to escape it will be even worse. We *torture* you before we cut off your head. Do you understand?"

They nodded, too shocked to say anything.

Ali then turned toward Lewis, who had been stripped naked and strapped to the beating post. Soft moans could be heard as he tried to mentally prepare himself for the beating. He didn't have long to wait. Ali put on thick leather gloves with rough edges at the knuckles, designed to cut deep into the flesh of anyone on the receiving end of his vicious blows. He hit the American again and again, each blow ripping flesh and imparting maximum pain. Lewis cried out as his head whipped back and forth, then backwards into the post. Blood oozed from his face and down the back of his neck.

"Now that you know your fate if you lie to us, let us talk about your secrets."

Lewis answered every question, making up what he didn't know. He described routes taken by the trucks from his camp; pickup and delivery points; type of load carried and how to tell when it was valuable or could be useful to the terrorists. He admitted to being a spy and signed the document of betrayal they placed before him—proof that would justify his capture and ultimate death to the world. They recorded it all.

Lewis' total cooperation was rewarded. He was removed from the post, handed his clothes and placed in the forward cage away from the other prisoners, where he was given an extra ration of bread and water. He looked across at the

other prisoners with tears in his eyes, not knowing whether
to eat the food or not. Murdock, sensing his dilemma,
nodded, and Lewis quickly gulped down the meager
nourishment.

Ali sat next to the informant to rest before beating the
next hostage. Had Lewis not cooperated so easily, Ali would
have continued to beat him into unconsciousness. He would
have been returned to the main cell without his clothes. His
turn would come up again and then again until a confession
was obtained.

This process ultimately coerced confessions from
everyone, leaving the prisoners feeling helpless. The rest of
the day would see each prisoner taken from the cage to be
beaten. Their captors continued to lock the cell in the same
menacing way, reinforcing the fact that there would be
absolutely no opportunity for escape.

ℜ

By mid afternoon the old guys sat on the side of the road
exhausted, taking only their third break of the day to drink
some water and eat a bit more of the dog meat for
nourishment. It had already been a long day, but they knew
that they needed to travel as far as they could before dark.

Owens started to become suspicious that their
surroundings were quiet — too quiet. Not even a bird could
be heard.

Suddenly, shots rang out, some kicking up dirt barely a
yard away. Owens spun quickly and realized that they had
been surrounded. A dozen very ugly and treacherous

looking men stepped out from behind the bushes and shouted at them. Several had fired rifles to get their attention—it had worked. The man who appeared to be in charge swaggered toward the tired group. He had two belts of ammunition crisscrossed over his chest, looking more like Pancho Villa without a sombrero than he did a bandit from the Middle East.

He spoke in Persian—Farsi as the English speaking countries referred to it—which uses many Arabic words that were added to the Iranian language when Islam was introduced in 641 AD. Jabaar understood him and immediately put his hands in the air, leaving his rifle on the ground. The rest of the group, although not understanding a word, followed his actions. The leader told Jabaar something else, and Jabaar put his knife down next to his rifle.

This wasn't good. Owens could see they were outnumbered two to one—and that didn't even count the fact that his group was practically unarmed. They had been caught by surprise with no chance to defend themselves.

The leader spoke again and Jabaar responded. They exchanged some brief dialogue before he directed his comments to the entire group. In broken English he stated, "We bandits. We tie you up, then take money. We not hurt you."

"No fuckin' way." Owens took a step toward the leader. "I'll give you my money, but you're not tying me up."

Owens knew that if they were tied up, no matter what the promises, they would be completely vulnerable to their whims. These men could do anything they wanted, including torture them, and there would be nothing they could do about it. He would fight to his death, but would make sure he did it on his terms—with his hands free.

The leader looked quizzically at Jabaar, who explained what Owens had said, adding that they didn't have much money. The bandit shrugged. "Maybe we just shoot you now, be done with it."

He nodded at his men, and they closed in tighter around the old guys, raising their rifles. "You will kneel…now!"

Jabaar and the others fell to their knees. Owens remained standing.

"That mean you too!" The leader hit him in the stomach with the butt of his rifle.

Owens fell to the ground gasping for breath. The leader put the barrel of his rifle against his head; his men did the same with the others.

"They Americans. Should we vote what we do to them?"

The bandits laughed. Very funny. Vote, just like Americans.

One of them said, "I vote to kill the little one first." He gestured at Jabaar.

Another said, "No, I vote to tie them up and leave them to die."

"More fun to kill them first, *then* leave them to die."

Everyone laughed, then an argument ensued as to who should be the first to die. They decided that Owens should go first because he'd challenged their leader; he had a bad attitude.

Owens looked up at the leader and said, "Hold on a minute. What country are we in?"

"What country? Iran. Where you think?"

Gulping for breath Owens said, "Listen. We are trying to help friends. Iraqi rebels have 'em. We need to find where they've taken 'em fast, or all of us will wind up dead."

"You dead right now." His men laughed.

"We mean you no harm. We'll leave Iran as soon as we get 'em back."

The leader shook his head. "You and these old men try rescue friends from armed Iraqis?"

"Yes."

"You in luck today. We *hate* Iraqi terrorists; especially ones sneak across border into our country. We glad Saddam Hussein gone. He evil. If I see Iraqis first, I kill them myself, release your friends."

"Why don't you help us then?"

"We not interfere. It your problem."

"Do you have any wheels we could use?"

"Wheels?"

"You know, a truck or something we could borrow?"

The leader shook his head. "No wheels for you."

"How about some food or water then?"

"You brave to ask. We give you some. But we still want money...now."

Owens and the others reached into their pockets and pulled out everything they had, handing it over to the leader. What were they going to need money for anyway? It was of no use to them out here.

The bandits gave them water and a small amount of food. "This all we can spare. If you need more, how you Americans say it? You shit out of luck."

He started to walk away, then turned and said, "There maybe not be any other bandits out here, but if any stop you, tell them you already been robbed by me, the famous *Shah of Iran*."

All the bandits laughed as they disappeared into the brush.

Owens shrugged. "Man, am I out of practice. That type of ambush would never have happened to me in the Marines *or* the Army. I've got to pay more attention."

Johnson said, "You were in the Army too? You never mentioned *that* before."

"Just for two years. I was drafted out of school. After my stint in Vietnam I knew the military would be my life, but as a Marine, not as a soldier. Nothin against 'em, I just knew I wanted to be a Marine. Come on, let's go. We're burning daylight."

ℜ

"No word from Camp Mojave all day?"

Tom Randall was noticeably upset as Skip Schick, his administrative assistant, updated him late in the afternoon upon his return.

"I didn't expect to hear from anyone over the weekend. I was just out there Saturday. Now you tell me they were supposed to have delivered supplies to over three dozen stores today, and didn't show up at a single one? I've seen delays before, but this is ridiculous."

Schick nodded. "I know. I talked with a couple of 'em on the road Saturday morning. They were excited about a poker game that night with the consultant. I had to find Johnson a new shooter. Nothing seemed strange. You know the land line is still down."

"Something's wrong out there. I've got to find out what it is before reporting to Corporate. We'll go out there first thing in the morning."

It was standard procedure for civilians moving throughout Iraq to travel in at least a two-car convoy with drivers, usually locals who were trained and trusted, and a shooter skilled in firearms. Although traveling east into what was considered a much safer region than Baghdad, safety precautions were followed as a matter of course. This included the wearing of a flak jacket and metal helmet by each traveler within the two vehicles.

"You got it, Boss. What time do you want to leave?"

"No later than seven. It will take several hours with all the checkpoints, and I want us to be there before noon."

"You want *me* to go with you?" Schick rarely left the office, much less ventured out into the suburbs of Baghdad. He believed that if he stayed close to home, someday he'd be able to *go* home...his own home back in the States. He admitted it to himself with a smile: he was a chicken Schick.

"Do you have a problem with that?"

"Uh-uh. But shouldn't someone stay here, like me, in case they call in or something?"

"What good would that do? You wouldn't be able to call me anyway, not after I pass the halfway mark. You know cell phones don't work that far out."

"No problem. I'll take care of everything. See you at seven."

Randall did not respond. He was already thinking about what he might find out at the camp. Communications had always been a problem that far out. Cell phones didn't work very well anywhere in Baghdad, but that situation was improving. They didn't work at all at Camp Mojave. Terrorists from neighboring countries and insurgents from within were continually cutting down landlines all over Iraq, and the one that connected them to Camp Mojave had not been operative for several days.

He knew there was a good crew out there, even if some of them were old. They still performed well in spite of having to endure the continual hazing of some of the younger men. The older men were steady in their approach to things. You could always count on them. The other guys could learn something from them, if they'd take the time to listen. Since arriving in camp they had submitted a lot of good ideas for improvement, many on the drawing board for implementation.

Schick suddenly ran back into Randall's office frantically shouting, "Boss, turn on the TV. You gotta see this!"

On the Fox News station, his drivers could be seen on their knees, bound with duct tape. Armed masked men stood around them. The leader said that he represented al-Qaeda and that unless Iraqi prisoners were released, these captives would be killed one by one, each day starting on Friday, January 13th. They had thirteen hostages—twelve drivers, one consultant.

"Thirteen? What about the rest?"

Randall knew he had seventeen drivers out there plus the consultant. What had happened to the other five? Had they already been killed? Which ones? Were they killed in the attack? And how did the terrorists know that one was a consultant? He couldn't fathom that piece of information being volunteered by anyone. He'd been afraid something horrible like this had happened—it was the only answer. He also realized that Friday was just four days away.

Then something unexpected was said that impacted the trucking company just as much as the loss of its drivers. The speaker went on to say that if the government wouldn't let the Iraqi prisoners go, the lives of the hostages could still be saved with the payment of one million dollars for each one held. A total of thirteen million dollars, no later than Friday. After describing how they were to be contacted when they had the money, the screen went black.

CNN ran the same footage, as did the Al-Jaazera Network, with people in neighboring countries running into the streets and celebrating. The talking heads discussed the possibilities of what might happen next, along with their consequences, none of which sounded good. Neither the U.S.-led coalition nor the new Iraqi government was going to set any of the Iraqi prisoners free. That would never be considered, and they knew the terrorists were already aware of that. This was just an excuse for the militants to publicly kill more Americans and justify it with their spy charges. They would show the world, maybe even convince more Iraqis that they were in charge—no one else but them.

Randall knew he couldn't go to Corporate for money yet because there were still too many unanswered questions. At least he now had an idea as to what had happened out at the camp. He told Schick, "We still need to go out there and see what happened. Damn that curfew. We could go right now. First thing in the morning…you and me, buddy."

"Right. Good night, Boss."

ℜ

After leaving the bandits, the old guys walked until dusk before finding a protected spot to spend the night. There had been no sign of the truck except for tire tracks. They knew that they couldn't go much farther. They had rationed water all day and still had a full bottle left. For dinner they ate the rest of the dog meat and some of what little the bandits had given them. That was it. They ate it cold, too tired to dig another hole for a fire.

"Rodney, you've never told us the real story about how you wound up here," Jacobs said. "What all did you do wrong?"

"Well, I already told you I was a conscientious objector during the Vietnam War. Sorry Dave, I know that pisses you off so I don't brag about it. It's just the way it was."

"You're right, but that's my problem, not yours."

"I was one of the first to go up to Canada to avoid the draft. Part of the hippie movement I guess, but without the VW bus and flowers. I smoked a lot of pot though, and still think it should be legalized. It could be so much cheaper than booze, especially when you grow it yourself... Not that I've ever done anything like that."

"Yeah, right!" They all laughed.

"When I finally came back, I was way out of touch, even with a Political Science teaching degree. Many school administrators were sympathetic to my cause, but some thought that I had been a traitor for not serving my country."

"There you go!"

"I know, Dave. But that hadn't crossed my mind when I headed north. I just didn't believe in violence and didn't understand why we needed to be in Vietnam. It seemed like such a waste of lives, and I didn't want to be part of the waste. So I left. I had a point to make to society, and I was damn well going to make it. I met Judy in Canada. She camped out and smoked pot with us, and didn't think the

U.S. should be in Vietnam either. She was perfect for me, so we got married.

"I've never stayed anywhere for long, moving from job to job. I think I've had a chip on my shoulder since then, and that hasn't helped me keep a job. After I was fired this last time I couldn't find any more work and really went over the edge when we ran out of money. I started smoking more than usual. But to make matters worse, I screwed around on Judy when I was stoned. I can't even remember how many women I woke up with the next morning. I never saw 'em again, but that didn't change anything. I still cheated on her.

"For a while, Judy accepted my lies about where I had been all night because she hated confrontations. But when I had to tell her I had VD, she got so mad that she kicked me out. Said to call her if I ever got my life back together, that she really loved me, but enough was enough. I still couldn't find a job and really needed money now, with two homes to support. So I got this job…in spite of my age.

"I've never shot a gun or killed anything in my life, other than that wild dog. I don't know how much help I can be. This whole thing scares me to death. And as bad a life as I have lived, I don't want to die. And I don't want any of you to die because I let you down. The thought of that scares me even more."

"Listen Rodney," Owens said, "your past is a lot different than mine, and I won't even try to understand it. But you need to know that there are two types of killing. There is *proactive* killing, and that's what criminals do. Then there's *protective* killing. That's when you are forced to defend yourself or your family and friends from harm. That's what we'll be doing, killing to protect others who were captured by proactive killers. There's no way we can let them succeed."

Numley scowled as he thought about the consequences of their endeavor. "What the hell are we doing over here in the first place? It reminds me of Vietnam. The only difference is we actually won *this* war, but only the invasion part. We seem to be losing all the other wars being fought in the streets. There weren't any weapons of mass destruction so we should have let well enough alone. I'm sorry Jabaar, but you and your people should have solved this problem yourselves. We'll never get out of this mess."

Jacobs shrugged. "A lot of people wonder why we're over here. None of us have all the answers, but I think the world is better off without Saddam Hussein. Sure, we never found the weapons that many thought were here, but we did find labs that were making 'em. And don't forget, it only takes a regular-sized briefcase to hide enough of that chemical shit to wipe out a whole city. Something that small could still be here, or easily smuggled out. We know he tested it on his own people, so he did have it at one time and wasn't afraid to use it. And he *was* supporting terrorists all over the world with millions of dollars, so I say, good riddance."

Numley added, "Don't get me wrong, the war on terror is one thing, but I do object to this Iraqi war. We should have sent better negotiators to talk through the issues. And I still think that if it weren't for the oil, we wouldn't be here."

"You could be right," Jacobs said. Our economy runs on oil. But there *are* other reasons, and isn't it better to be fighting them over here instead of fighting 'em in the states? New Yorkers know that better than all of us, and that was just the 9/11 attack. Nobody likes war. But if the terrorists prevail in the Middle East, then come to the states, do you really think they will be willing to negotiate when they are geared up to kill us all? That's their goal, you know. There's nothing else going for them. They live in abject poverty, something that won't change even if they ruled the world. They'll just drag us survivors down to their level."

"Well, the Iraqis need to take control of their own destiny sooner, rather than later. America can't stay here forever," Numley replied.

Johnson added, "You're right about that. And we need other countries to help eliminate terrorists in their part of the world to make this all worthwhile. These radical Muslims say it's in the name of Allah. How can anyone think God would condone such vicious actions? They're destroying what He has created! How can *that* please Him?"

Owens reminded them that Muslim extremists had been terrorizing the world, including the U.S., for years, and that it didn't just start on 9/11. He mentioned Sirhan Sirhan, a Muslim extremist who assassinated Bobby Kennedy in 1968; the athletes that were killed at the 1972 Olympic games in Munich; the Iranian U.S. embassy hostages held for over a year in 1979; the U.S. Marine barracks in Beirut that was blown up in 1983; the hijacked cruise ship *Achille Lauro* and the killing of a crippled 70-year-old civilian passenger just because he was an American; the two planes full of civilians that were hijacked and blown up in the eighties. "And in 1993 they bombed the World Trade Center for the first time. Almost all of these casualties have been civilian."

Johnson nodded. "That's when we heard the name Osama bin Laden for the first time. The 9/11 attack was like Pearl Harbor in 1941...it was the one that pissed us off enough to finally fight back."

"The goal of Muslim extremists is a broad Islamic state centered in Iraq before expanding into neighboring countries," Jacobs said. "If they lose here, they will appear weak to others they hope to recruit for their cause. And in spite of their large numbers, Muslims will have lost their credibility as a world power. This is why we have to stop them here.

"The attack on Fallujah, for example, was a great secondary success for our troops. All the strategists predicted it would take months to neutralize. Once they got the green light, it only took them two weeks to flush out most of terrorists. It was a textbook battle, and although it didn't sound like it from the news reports, the number of bombings actually decreased after the terrorists lost that stronghold."

"That right. It much quieter after that," Jabaar said.

As they settled down for some much needed sleep, Johnson said, "You know Dave, I've been meaning to ask you something. You mentioned that you were in the Army in Vietnam. I thought you were only in the Marines. My brother was in the Army too. Jonathan Johnson. You didn't happen to meet him over there, did you?"

"Johnnie Johnson was your brother? We were in the same squad when he was gunned down." He bowed his head. "I liked him a lot."

"All we got was his tags and an American flag. Never really heard what happened. Did he die quick?"

"Yeah. He was group leader...up front when we were hit. Died that same day. He never knew what happened."

"That's a relief. We always wondered."

"He was a brave man, Charlie. I was proud to follow him."

"Thanks Dave." He turned over and fell asleep.

Owens stayed awake for several hours after learning that Charlie was Johnnie's brother. It brought back memories of that deadly attack, and how he had tried to save his life by dragging him back to cover. He had grieved over the loss of *that* life. It was the first of many he would witness. Then, he thought about how much he had enjoyed his brief retirement and what had led up to his involvement in Iraq.

It had started out so harmlessly—but ended up so regrettably, resulting in his sudden need for money—just like the others…

ℜ

Retired for almost five years, Dave Owens spent his entire life serving his country in the military. He had even called the Camp Pendleton commander to help in the attack on Afghanistan in 2002, but was told his services were no longer needed. When he saw the ad for drivers in Iraq after his need for money had surfaced, he decided he could get back in action helping his country and earn big bucks too.

The dilemma started during a surprise visit to his son from a long-ago marriage and seven-year old grandson in Southern California. Owens had retired to a trailer park in the High Sierra Mountains, close to a babbling stream and a lake full of fish. The fish diet kept him lean; the daily hiking kept him fit. It was an all-day drive south, which was why he seldom saw his family. But little Davy had been sick, even hospitalized. He needed to see him.

As he drove up the long circular driveway, Davy saw him coming and was already opening the front door as his grandfather got out of his car. He squealed with glee as Owens showed him the GI Joe set he had just purchased, racing into the house with his new possession.

As he retrieved the housewarming flowers a voice said, "Uncle Dave...it's been a long time."

The redheaded girl in jeans and a baggy sweatshirt was barefoot. She stood about five and a half feet tall and appeared to be in her late teens. Owens didn't have a clue as to who she was.

"You don't recognize me? I'm Molly. I met you six years ago at their old house. I was only fifteen then.

"The next door babysitter, right? What are you doing way over here?"

"Still babysitting. They left this morning for a short vacation and have never found another sitter. I'm out of school right now with no plans, so here I am."

"So much for my surprise. Now what?"

"Well, let's see...spend time with Davy? He idolizes you."

Davy returned and asked his grandpa to play soldier with him. As Owens followed, Molly said she was fixing dinner and asked if he drank wine. His son had given her a large bottle to celebrate her twenty-first birthday that weekend. "After you play for a while, I'll feed Davy his favorite macaroni and cheese. Then we can put him to bed before we eat."

Two hours later, the house was finally quiet. As they sat down to eat, Owens raised his glass. "Here's to my new friend Molly. May this birthday be your best ever and that you live the rest of your life as if there is no tomorrow, just in case tomorrow never comes."

"Is that how you live your life, Uncle Dave?"

"Pretty much. I've done what I've wanted to do...without breaking any laws of course. I'm content with my life. How about you?"

"It's OK."

Molly said that he was a hero to her too; his son had told her about all the things he had done in the war. She thanked him for calling her a friend. "It's a real honor to be considered a friend by you, Uncle Dave."

"And please, just call me Dave...now that you're...older."

They fell silent as they ate. As Molly had limited experience drinking anything alcoholic, she drank her first glass of wine in several gulps. Owens explained that it should be sipped leisurely to enjoy its flavor. Her second and third glass went down more slowly, as did the fourth. Not wanting her to drink alone, he matched her glass for glass. The bottle was almost empty as they finished their meal, and Molly had become quite talkative. She cleared the table, checked in on Davy and then joined Owens on the patio to finish their last glass of wine.

The thought of spending an entire weekend playing with a seven-year-old kid and entertaining a babysitter didn't sound all that attractive to Owens. He wondered if there were any fish in a nearby pond. Teaching Davy how to fish would be OK.

The evening was balmy and the dining room chandelier provided enough light to fill the patio with a soft glow. As they looked up at the stars, Owens noticed something. "What's that over there?"

"That's the Jacuzzi. I love to lounge in it with the warm, but not too hot, jets beating on my back. How hot do you like it, Dave?"

"I take showers, not baths. Never been in one."

"Well then, tonight's the night. Let's jump in right now. You can really relax."

"I'm pretty relaxed right now. And besides, I didn't bring my swimming trunks."

"Do you have anything on underneath your jeans?"

"Just my boxers."

She jumped up and said, "That'll work!"

They removed the cover together. Owens paused, not quite knowing what to do next. Molly grabbed the bottom of her sweatshirt and pulled it up over her head. She wasn't wearing a bra. And although she didn't have large breasts, they were nicely shaped with tiny red nipples that glistened in the soft light. Owens, caught by surprise, could only gawk at her. He hadn't been with a woman for a while and had forgotten how beautiful breasts could be close up.

"Are you still just standing there? Come on, catch up, silly!"

She took off her jeans and climbed into the tub. Owens stared again, this time at her thong panties that didn't leave much to the imagination. He took off everything but his shorts and quickly followed her into the water. He didn't want her to see that the sight of her almost completely naked body had caused some excitement in his own.

They sank deep into the water and let the hot bubbles completely envelop them. It was soothing as the stream of water from the jets bore into their backs, relaxing each muscle in its path.

"So this is what a Jacuzzi is all about!"

"Fantastic isn't it?"

"Make sure I don't fall asleep and drown in here, OK?"

"Don't worry, Dave, I'll keep my eyes on you. Can I ask you a personal question?"

"Sure, why not?"

"How old were you when you first made love to a woman?"

"Man, when you say personal you do mean personal, don't you?" He paused a moment before answering. "I don't know if you would count this or not, but I was still in school. We didn't go all the way. That didn't happen until after I graduated. But I felt like we were making love. Does that count?"

"It depends. What did you do?"

"Well, we kissed and snuggled for hours. I had a lot of respect for that girl and didn't want to offend her. I really cared for her; in fact, I think I was in love with her, but who knows at that age. She once told me she wasn't a prude, but I still didn't want to take a chance on making her mad—or pregnant—so I didn't try anything. I think I had her on a pedestal."

"Well, now that it's midnight, I just officially turned twenty-one and still haven't gone all the way yet. Some guys have groped me and were ticked off when I said I wasn't that kind of a girl. I want to make love with someone tender…like you seem to be…someone who would be gentle and caring rather than just trying to score with a virgin."

"Someone will come along for you, Molly. You just have to give it time."

"I feel like I *have* given it time. Would you...mind holding me a few minutes and pretend that you care? It would mean a lot to me."

"Well, I do care. You are one of the nicest girls I have ever met. But under the circumstances — "

Molly didn't wait for him to finish. She slid over and wrapped her arms around him. Her nipples pressed against his chest and like before, excitement surged through his body. His breath quickened in response to her nearness. She pulled back and looked at him, then kissed him on the lips, gently at first, then with full passion. She drew his tongue inside her mouth, where it flicked against her teeth before going even deeper. Then she let out a small gasp as he reached up and cupped her breast with his hand, tenderly pinching her nipple between his thumb and forefinger. She rolled on top of him, her thigh between his legs, and rubbed it back and forth on his hardness.

"No matter what happens tonight, this is already the best birthday I've ever had!" she exclaimed.

They made love under the stars until almost sunup, leaving the Jacuzzi for the master bedroom before they finally fell asleep with those same stars shining brightly through its big bay window.

Owens stayed for two more days. He left on Monday morning after Davy went to school, deciding not to wait until his son and daughter-in-law returned. He didn't think he could carry on a conversation with them and keep a straight face. In fact, he didn't know if he would *ever* be able to wipe the grin off his face. He was a happy man and she was definitely a happy young woman.

Owens drove away knowing he'd never see her again. Sadness fell over him, but one he knew had to be endured. It wasn't until nine months later that he learned she was pregnant. His son told him that she was going to have a baby any day, and that she wasn't married, so she would have to raise the child alone. Her folks were upset, but she wouldn't tell anyone the name of the father. They would help her until she graduated from college, but then she would be on her own. That was when he decided to go back to work and earn a lot of money quickly to help her out. He called Tiger Trucking Company that afternoon.

Day Four – Tuesday, January 10th

THEY STARTED OUT at daybreak again to get the blood flowing and warm up after another cold night. How much farther would they have to go? They had driven or walked over a hundred miles since leaving Camp Mojave three nights ago. Their needs were immediate. They had to find water...today. Even with the extra food supplied by the bandits, they would eventually need more—but not today.

By mid-morning Numley had become exhausted by the continued physical exertion and wove wearily back and forth across the road. Owens had reluctantly decided they needed to stop and rest when the tire tracks suddenly disappeared, right in the middle of the road. Charlie Johnson scratched his head wondering what the hell had happened. It was as if it had been scooped up into a black hole. An old naval salt would say it was the work of a skyhook.

Jacobs moved farther on down the road to see if he could pick up the tracks again. Owens went into the bushes. He started on the left side, but found nothing. After crossing to the other side he discovered Numley's truck behind the brush that had been piled high all around it. He summoned the others as Jacobs returned with news that he had picked up tracks all right, but they didn't belong to any tires. They were boot tracks...and lots of them.

They gathered around the truck, at first assuming it had finally run out of gas. But, by using a tree branch as a dipstick, they discovered it still had about two inches of fuel.

"What do you think, Rodney?" Johnson said. "Enough gas to go another forty or fifty miles?"

"Maybe even a little farther. I didn't know there was that much in there."

"So running out of gas wasn't the reason it stopped," Owens said.

"It was acting up the past couple of weeks; you know, sputtering at times, but it kept running and I just kept forgetting to get it fixed."

Johnson started to climb aboard. "Let's see what I can do with it."

Owens stopped him. "What do you have in mind?"

"Well, I think it's an electrical problem." He turned to Numley. "Acted up but never stopped, just sputtered, right Rodney?"

"Yeah, like it was about to stop, but never did."

"So completely dieing like it did—well now, that's a new symptom. I've fixed many a truck with a couple of screwdrivers and my adjustable wrench. Always kept that and good ole duct tape in a bag under the front seat of my truck."

"Can something like that be fixed without those tools?" Owens asked.

"Doubt it."

"Damn."

"But why try when I brought em with me?" He took out a small bag from his coat pocket and held them up. "I grabbed em when *my* truck quit on us the other day. With these tools, I'll bet I could get 'er running again in an hour or so."

"You'll get your chance, but not now. We need to move on. They might be real close. We don't want them to hear the truck, or worse, come up on them too fast. Either one and we're dead meat."

Reluctantly, they agreed. They didn't know how much farther they had to go, but now at least both groups were on foot. And the group in front would be like a herd of cattle, presumably traveling much slower. The sooner they started following the boot tracks, the sooner they might find the others.

ℜ

Tom Randall looked at what used to be his trucker camp in shock. Completely destroyed. The buildings had been flattened, the trucks now just piles of rubble. Everything had been blown to bits, the pieces lying next to — and on top of — the remains of dead Iraqi guards out in the bushes.

They had been taken by surprise. He knew all along it was a mistake to hire civilians to guard these camps. But corporate headquarters had the bright idea it would provide jobs for the locals, and — oh yes — it would save the company money. The bottom-line again. Professional guards would cost a lot more, but in hindsight it would have been well worth the price.

From what Randall could see, the only dead bodies were those of Iraqi guards. No drivers. Although he couldn't be sure. Scavengers had mutilated their bodies over the past several days. Uniforms provided the only clue as to who they were. He wondered what had happened to the missing five drivers, and equally important, who were they?

Several members of the Marine NCIS unit were already at the site, investigating the devastation. Randall walked up to the officer in charge and asked what his people knew or suspected so far. He was told that they had been investigating the campsite throughout the morning. The throats of all the guards had been slit, so they were likely neutralized without firing a shot. After counting the bodies, Randall knew that two of the guards were unaccounted for, according to his records, and based on the uniforms, one was Colonel Abdul. The thought was that they were either able to escape or were taken prisoner as well. He hoped it was the former, and that they would eventually show up to fill in the blanks. As two trucks were also missing, it was assumed they were used to transport the prisoners to their hideout. The most recent tracks led to the main highway where they could not be followed any farther. Based on this observation, it was assumed they headed back toward Baghdad and could be hiding anywhere along that one hundred-mile stretch of desolate road.

"Are there any other bodies out here?" Randall asked. "They only had thirteen hostages. Five of my men are unaccounted for."

"No sir. All are Iraqi. Although badly chewed up, they were mostly young. Killed by their own people...people of the same faith...people who think they are doing good by killing their own. What a shame."

"Yes, and I knew all of these boys. Most of them took this job to earn money to support their families. And we could only get a thousand dollars of insurance on each of them because of the cost. That will help for a while, then they're back where they started—minus a contributing member of the family, of course. How long are you going to be out here, Captain?"

"Looks like the rest of the day. A detail will be here shortly to pick up the bodies for identification purposes and return them to their families for proper burial..."

"Captain, come over here, I want you to see something," one of his men called.

"What is it, Corporal?"

"An explosive device that didn't go off! This one is very simple in design...a small clock tied to several sticks of dynamite. I can't believe this is the only type of explosive they used to level the camp. The most common is C-4...it only takes twenty pounds to blow a house apart. But it's highly volatile, so while it is popular, a lot of amateurs get killed using it. Either these guys are amateurs, or they are low on money."

"Why didn't it explode?"

"Simple, sir. The clock stopped. It never reached the time set to detonate the dynamite. I've already pulled out the wires so it won't go off by accident."

"Good work, Corporal. Let's get it back to the lab so we can try to find out where this stuff came from."

Another noncom walked up and said, "Captain, we just found another body, and this one isn't Iraqi."

Randall groaned. "Oh no. Let me see if I can identify him."

"His face is disfigured. He was shot though, not stabbed, I can tell you that."

"Shit!" Randall closed his eyes. "Shit, shit, shit."

After he calmed down, Randall thanked the officer for the information and asked to be kept in the loop. Now that he knew more of the details, he could contact headquarters with an update and learn what their plans were for getting his men released. He turned to his assistant and said, "Let's get back to Baghdad and make sure all the right people are working on this! The boys back in the states aren't going to like my recommendation."

ℜ

By noon their water was gone. They had traveled all morning without rest, except for the time spent with Numley's truck. Worse, they were still following boot tracks. They thought they'd have found the men by now. This looked hopeless. They were going to have to stop and find water, and that might take the rest of the day — valuable time lost.

As Owens and Jacobs started to discuss their options, the tracks disappeared. This time, however, they were between two large hills with nowhere to hide anything...or anyone.

Johnson said, "Can you believe this? What the hell's happening—?"

The sound of a vehicle coming toward them interrupted him.

"Out of sight, everybody. Follow me!" Owens exclaimed.

He led them through a small opening between some bushes on the right side of the road. Moments later a small open bed truck with only a driver appeared. The man wore camouflaged military fatigues. The truck bed contained supplies—several cans of gasoline, water, boxes of food, and other items. The driver stopped between the two hills, turned off the engine and called out, "Allahu Akbar."

"What did he say?" Owens whispered to Jabaar.

"God is great."

Two men emerged from behind the bushes on the other side, looked up and down the road, and then pushed the brush aside. The old guys immediately saw the entrance to a large cave; it had been completely hidden by the foliage. The driver started the truck and drove into the cave. The tire tracks were swept away, the brush pulled back in place behind the other men. Clearly, they had found where the terrorists had taken their captives.

Johnson sighed. "Was that close or what? And if we had decided to hide on *that* side of the road? We'd have been toast."

"But you followed me, didn't you! Let that be a lesson." Owens laughed to himself as he thought how lucky they were that he had made the right decision. He needed them to follow his commands without question. Luck or not, this example would serve as a reminder of his expertise under extreme conditions when a split-second decision had to be made.

The truck remained in the cave for a long time. The old guys waited impatiently. Finally, one of the terrorists emerged from the bushes and looked around. Once satisfied, he signaled the others, and the brush was again pushed aside. Soon the driver was on his way in the now-empty truck, and the cave again disappeared.

"Looks like they've thought of everything," Owens muttered.

He led them through the foliage up the hill, always keeping the cave's entrance in their sights. Arriving at the top, they found themselves half a football field away from the entrance, with plenty of cover. "Although we haven't seen anyone, they might have a lookout over there. We need to stay quiet and keep out of sight. Understood?"

In less than an hour they had learned not only where the terrorists hid, but also that they had help from the outside with supplies delivered to their doorstep.

Owens moved away from the others. He needed to be alone so he could think things through. What a mess. They were undoubtedly the only ones who knew where the hostages were being held. But at the same time, he realized how impossible the situation had become. Attacking a building to stage a rescue was one thing. Trying to pull them from the confines of a cave was a different matter, a challenge he had never experienced or even contemplated. It dramatically changed the odds in favor of the enemy. For the first time in his life he began to question himself and his ability to complete a task. He couldn't let the others see his uncertainty, or they would be beaten before they began. The lingering question: were he and his men strong enough and savvy enough to devise a plan that would work without getting everyone killed? One thing for sure: they first had to survive themselves, and at the moment that was questionable.

ℜ

After a much-needed rest, Jacobs and Numley, with Jabaar in the lead, left to search for water. Owens directed them to find an area that would be out of sight from a potential terrorist lookout. He had already decided they would take turns watching the cave entrance. He took the first watch while Johnson reclined and elevated his injured leg.

It took a couple of hours to find water, but Jabaar again succeeded. The location was in a ravine on the other side of the hill, a quarter-mile away. The sand was soft and the three of them were able to uncover the water in half the time as before. They quenched their thirst, and then returned to the others with full bottles.

With the water problem solved, Owens decided that they needed to explore the hill that contained the cave. "We'll meet at the top, working our way around each side to get there. I still haven't seen any lookouts, so they might just be a bit overconfident. But, be careful."

They divided into two teams, Owens and Numley on one and Johnson and Jabaar on the other. Johnson had insisted on going, in spite of his even more noticeable limp. Jacobs stayed behind to watch the entrance.

They spent the next hour carefully searching the area, finally meeting near the top of the rocky hill, discouraged that they hadn't found anything for their efforts. "Hey gang," Johnson whispered, "look what I found."

He indicated a hole that went straight down into the hill. Its width was about two feet in diameter, and it was well hidden by some large rocks and brush strategically placed there along with dirt for an authentic look. It would have been missed completely, except that Johnson, moving slower than the rest, almost stumbled into it.

An exhaust hose snaked out of the hole from what they assumed was some kind of engine running below. Because of its location, they determined that the hole went down into the back of the cave, and that the engine was probably running an electrical generator. Because they couldn't hear anything, they figured that the generator was likely equipped with a muffler and encased in an insulated box.

"It's dangerous to run one of those things in an enclosed area like a cave because of the fumes," Johnson said as he stepped next to the hole and reached down to touch the hose. "This here takes care of that problem."

Owens pulled him back. "Stay away from the hole, Charlie. Someone might hear you, or you might kick a rock down there."

Then he noticed a strip of wire covered by dirt, which led to a small tree with an antenna secured at the top.

"Might be how they communicate to the outside," Jabaar said.

Johnson shook his head. "Maybe. But it looks more like a TV antenna to me...something that receives signals, not sends them. But you never know."

The discovery of the hole provided Owens with another option to consider. Its diameter was enough for a man to climb down. At the moment, he didn't know if that made any sense, but it was something to think about. He started feeling better about their situation. That just might work. They couldn't climb down there during the day, as it would be too light with the generator on. But at night, when hopefully most would be asleep and the lights out...now that was a different story.

Owens decided that one of them would remain there during the day to keep an eye on the hole. Located just over the top of the hill, it could not be seen from their vantage point on the other side. He wanted to know if anyone ever used the hole to get in or out. They would also continue to watch the cave entrance from the opposite hill. It was important to learn of the terrorists' movements before making any final rescue plans.

As he explained his strategy, Numley interrupted: "Isn't the exhaust coming out of this hose carbon monoxide? And if you breathe it, wouldn't it put you to sleep?"

Johnson said, "Yep, it sure would... permanently."

"So turning it back into the cave wouldn't work?"

"Not hardly...we'd wind up getting all of them killed — as well as us if we tried to go in there."

"Damn. I thought that might be a safer possibility."

Owens said, "Think it through a little more, guys. Your thoughts aren't that farfetched though, Rodney. You're just suggesting the wrong substance. The military has already developed calmative agents. They're gas sedatives that can be used in a small area like this cave that would put everyone to sleep, but without killing 'em. It would have been perfect for this. We'll just have to come up with another idea, that's all. Let's head back to camp."

ℜ

As Jacobs watched the entrance, he again rued the day he had decided to take this job. He couldn't get it out of his mind. He was not a yes man and was smart enough to know when senior leadership was headed in the wrong direction. Terminated twice for voicing his opinion about poor corporate decisions, he saw both companies go out of business within a year of his departure.

Then it happened again. The last company was so worried about doing something wrong that it never did anything right—at least from a sales perspective. You can't make chicken salad out of chicken shit, and that's what home office tried to do with a new, highly complicated retirement annuity. With a sales philosophy of *simple sells,* he knew they would never reach expected sales projections, and watched as senior management took what *was* a significant force in the market place and convert it into a non-entity over several short years. He refused to fail quietly and was ultimately asked to leave there as well. Because of his age, the request included a severance package along with some strings attached…a vow of silence. Before leaving, however, Jacobs did what most employees dreamed about—he told his boss to essentially take the job and shove it—that he wasn't welcome at his home and therefore would be excluded from attending the last annual dinner with his Western Division sales team. He smiled every time he thought about that last exchange with the asshole.

After many months of searching for another job without any luck, he told his wife Lynn, "Honey, I read about a high paying job driving a truck, so I called them."

"Driving a truck? Right. What did they say?"

"Well, they said I would only have to make a six-month commitment to qualify for full pay, a living allowance and free transportation to the site. The best part is we could make close to a hundred thousand dollars, and if I stay a whole year, it would be over twice that amount with eighty thousand of it income tax-free. That would be like earning almost three hundred thousand dollars before taxes for one year of work. It even comes with a front-end cash bonus."

"Sounds too good. What's the catch? And free transportation? What does that mean?"

"Well..." He paused. "...the job's in Iraq."

"No! No way. I won't let you go! It's too dangerous. You'll get yourself killed, then I'll be all alone. I can go back to work. We don't need the money that bad—"

"Look, this income will help pay off the house so we don't have to use our savings. By the time I get back, our investment in that health food grocery chain will start paying out. We'll be able to live comfortably the rest of our lives."

"That's what I'm worried about. How long will the rest of *your* life be working over there? We can make it. You don't need to do this! Something will turn up. Give it more time."

Jacobs reminded her, "Everything has fallen through. It's only because I'm older than all the interviewers."

"Honey, I love you. I don't want to lose you. We've both read the horror stories about Iraq." She started to cry.

"It's much safer now." Jacobs tried to downplay the dangers. He told her about highly trained guards in the truck he'd be driving and at the camp where he would be staying. He went on to say their delivery services were appreciated by almost everyone in that country now, as they knew the Americans were there to help, not take over their country. "I promise that I will be OK."

"You won't take *any* chances then?"

"You know me. I'm a coward when it comes to bloodshed. I'll be safe. Swear to God!"

Lynn looked at him for a minute without responding, then told him that while he was gone she would knit things like mittens or a scarf or something useful for him over there. He doubted that would ever happen, as she was so involved with political and charitable volunteer work. But he told her to send him the first item she knitted. It would be his keepsake.

"I hear it dips down below a hundred degrees sometimes...in the middle of the night, so I could use something made out of wool."

Then they laughed through the tears as they hugged each other. Jacobs was going. His mind was made up, and Lynn knew there would be no changing it. He didn't really want to leave her, not even for a day, but he took solace in the fact that the job would provide the money they would need for the rest of their lives. He wasn't going to let this opportunity pass them by.

ℜ

Ali left the informant and his minions talking excitedly among themselves after watching the TV broadcast of their demands. He needed time to contemplate all that had transpired the past several days.

He was pleased...very pleased. The first broadcast had let the Americans know who he and his men were, what they had done and what they wanted. It went well.

Everything was coming together exactly the way it had been envisioned, Allah be praised. Even the first delivery of supplies had arrived on time. He was especially pleased that they would be alternating the drivers each day in an attempt to deceive anyone in the village who might be watching them come and go.

The Americans were weaklings. As he had found out the day before, inflicting the least amount of pain got most of them to divulge important secrets. He had already learned much about their transportation system in just one day of beatings. His group would be able to exploit this information either after these prisoners were released—or after they were dead. He hoped the Americans would test his veracity so he could kill one of the captured drivers because the trucking company refused to send money. He would deliver the tape of that death in addition to the one who tried to escape so that both would be shown on television. He knew if he had his way, he'd kill them all no matter what the response. But if he did that, their future demands would never be met. Still, he thought, a small smile forming on his face, if they delay, then he couldn't be held accountable for following through on his threats.

The next few days would prove much to other followers. He and his men were destined to make a difference. The world would learn more about their cause, and that they had the might of Allah on their side. The Americans and the other invaders of his country had to leave the sacred land of Iraq so it could be ruled the way it had always been ruled, with the blessing of Allah. It could not be placed in the hands of an American puppet that crumbled whenever demands were made by that unclean nation of infidels. Many people may have voted, but that was not the way things were done in this ancient of countries. The new regime will never survive. He and his group would make sure of that!

ℜ

Dusk brought a penetrating cold. The old guys huddled together in their makeshift camp to further discuss what they had learned that day and to prepare for the night ahead.

By the time they gathered kindling, built the fire in a secluded location on the other side of the hill closer to their source of water, heated the food given them by the bandits, and then eaten, the blackness of the night enveloped them. Owens had gone to the top of the hill a few times to maintain his surveillance of the cave. He believed that one could never have too much information when formulating a plan as dangerous as theirs would have to be.

As he hadn't seen any light emanating from the cave after the sun set, he assumed the terrorists turned off their generator to avoid it being seen in the dark. They likely used minimal lighting to move around during the evening hours. Therefore, it was determined that the rescue effort would need to take place at night, as there would be less chance of discovery. No details yet, but Owens's initial thought was that some of them would need to drop down into the cave through the hole and attempt to take the terrorists by surprise from the rear. Surprise was the key element, not only for the tactical military advantage, but also to eliminate the potential for them to notify other terrorists providing support, assuming they did have a transmitter. Their goal would be swift neutralization of the enemy.

Owens also realized something else, and even though it was premature to be thinking about it at this juncture, it *was* on his mind. Assuming they were able to free the prisoners, only half the job was done. They had to figure out a way to get everyone safely back to Baghdad and the protection of their own military.

The initial plan was potentially far too dangerous for them to attempt, but as Owens explained, it was just a start in the thinking process. The actual plan would undoubtedly change as they learned more over the next several days through observation. For example, they had no rope to lower themselves into the cave. Without that, his plan wouldn't work. But, a rope could be made out of tree roots. He had done that while in the military. Therefore, they would have to dig up roots and make that rope.

In addition, they had to get inside the cave and check it out in as much detail as possible. They needed to know the layout and the enemy head count, to determine the viability of whatever plan they devised. He said that the only solution was to try and intercept the supply truck.

"Jabaar could then drive it in and look around while they offload supplies."

"You want me drive in there?"

"Yes. None of us could get away with it because we aren't Iraqi. Do you think you could do it?"

"Yes…I can do that if it needed."

Owens smiled. "Thank you. You've already done a lot for us and we appreciate it."

Jacobs added, "We're gonna need a believable reason why a new face is behind the wheel."

"We'll come up with something."

Owens continued to think out loud. "So…we need to make a rope so a bunch of out-of-shape guys can climb down a hole into a cave, but before they do, we need our innocent-looking guard here to look mean enough to fool the terrorists inside into thinking that he's one of them. That's all. Anyone see any problems?"

By midnight, even though short on details, they did have an initial rescue plan. They were tired and gratefully fell on their rough beds made out of foliage.

"Charlie, you still with us? I was asking you how much you knew about Iraq?" Numley asked.

Johnson, who had been nodding, rejoined the conversation, "I know a little about it, why?"

In an attempt to impress everyone, Numley started to spew his knowledge about the country. "Before I came over here I read up on it. I found out it was occupied by Britain during World War I, and didn't gain its independence until 1932. It wasn't even a republic until 1958. This country is the size of California with a population of twenty-five million, yet has wreaked havoc in this part of the world for years. And although mostly Muslim, each ethnic group wants to rule the others. That's why there's so much unrest."

"It's a mess over here," Owens said, "even though the invasion was a success and Hussein was captured."

"Well, you don't read about it in the newspapers or see it on television," Jacobs added, "but after they got him things started to improve over here. In fact, forty-seven countries re-established their embassies."

"Their educational facilities have improved the most," Numley said. "Three thousand schools have been renovated and close to four hundred are now under construction. Over four million children enrolled in primary school this past October alone.

"And they've got five Police Academies with over 3,500 new officers graduating every eight weeks to protect their own people—in spite of the fact that so many of them are killed by terrorists daily. That takes a lot of guts."

Looking through glazed eyes, bored with the data-dump, Johnson muttered, "Ya know, I really don't give a shit about this. Guts? We're the ones about to risk getting our asses shot off going into that cave. Now that takes guts! And we're old farts, already exhausted, but with more work to do to get ready."

Johnson said what everyone was thinking. He carefully straightened his injured leg and continued: "In spite of all this, I still think I'm the luckiest man alive. I'm sixty-three years old and have lived a great life, even with the polio I had when I was a kid. My wife Ruthie died last year, otherwise I wouldn't even be here. I did some crazy things after she passed away. But I couldn't help it. I missed her so much I just went nuts."

"What'd you do, Charlie?"

Johnson put his head down and said softly, "Well, for one thing, I got drunk on the job. Could have lost my license, but the company I'd been with the past thirty years said it was time for me to retire and go fishing. I owned my own truck, but they took away my routes. I didn't have any place to go. Hell, I'm a roadie. My enjoyment in life has always been on the highway. I tried to find another job, but they'd take one look at me and tell me to forget it. All they could see was a wrinkled old man with a potbelly and a bum leg. I had just about given up when I saw the ad about this gig. It sounded kinda desperate, so I thought maybe they were hard up enough to hire a guy like me, faults and all."

"Hell, you're the best damn driver of the bunch," Owens said. "The way you maneuvered the big rig into that narrow slot when they decided not to use it anymore was pure magic. You remember a couple of the others tried to get it in there, but finally gave up. It only took you one try."

"Thanks Dave. That means a lot coming from you. I knew if I did get a job, it would be different from before...what with Ruthie being gone and all. She was my partner. We drove all over the good ole U. S. of A together. I don't know how many times we made love in the back of our rig at some remote rest area. Some public places too, like

Mount Rushmore with the presidents looking down. That was a good one."

Everyone laughed with Charlie as he reminisced. He continued on with another story.

"After we got married, a whole lot of things changed."

Jacobs asked, "What could possibly change that fast, after knowing her for so long?"

"Well, it actually started that first night on our honeymoon. As I said before, I'd known Ruthie since junior high, but we didn't start dating until we were in high school. We decided to get married just as soon as we graduated. It was summer and hot, and my car wasn't air-conditioned. When we got to our hotel room, even though we were both scared, we took off our clothes as fast as we could just to be more comfortable. Ruthie took one look at me after I dropped my shorts and blurted out that the clinical tests were right—smoking does stunt a man's growth. Both of us paid for that joke. It took me over an hour to get up and running again."

"But that didn't answer how things changed for you, Charlie."

"Well, things changed because I never smoked another cigarette after that. Yep, quit smoking tobacco and started chewin' it the very next day. Ruthie always regretted that little joke of hers."

Johnson paused for a moment to take a breath. "Another time we were attending a Vegas trucking convention."

"There he goes again." Owens was chuckling, but ole Charlie didn't hear him.

"There weren't many women like Ruthie driving trucks in those days, but she was a pistol and everyone got a kick out of her. At the last minute they asked her to speak at one of the sessions. Her topic was how to fit in as a woman driver. Ruthie spent all night putting her thoughts down on paper so she wouldn't forget anything. But when she got up to speak she was so nervous she dropped her notes all over the floor. That would have ended it for most people, but not Ruthie. She just leaned into the microphone and said she was sorry for being so jittery, but she had given up beer for Lent and the whiskey was killing her! That brought down the house and she ad-libbed the rest of her talk."

Rodney asked, "Did any of this really happen, Charlie?"

"Some of it, I think. I've told these stories for so long now it seems like they did...but I can't say for sure.

"Pancreatic cancer got her one week after we found out what was ailing her. I was with her when she took her last breath. She said she would see me again in heaven, if I was lucky enough to get there. What a gal. Joked until the very end.

"After I buried her I tried to carry on, but it just wasn't the same and I got canned. I knew if they'd hire me, my experience would be valuable over here...not only driving trucks but also keeping 'em running. They never asked me how old I was, and I damn well didn't volunteer it. They hired me.

"I don't know...maybe what we're doin' right now will be a shortcut to seeing her again. I hope one of you will make sure I get buried next to her if I'm not around when this is over. She kidded about me not getting to heaven, but there's no way she's not already there. And I plan on joining her. You know what I mean?"

No one answered. By this time they were fast asleep.

Day Five – Wednesday, January 11th

JACOBS WOKE UP first, thankful for a full night's sleep. They had managed to adapt to the cold temperatures at night, along with sleeping on the ground. Their foliage mattresses weren't all that bad. Johnson was still snoring, which was good, as he'd had the most trouble sleeping. His leg seemed to bother him more at night than during the day when he could move around.

The first order of business was to make a rope. They started by digging up the roots of nearby trees. Unsure how deep the floor of the cave was, they estimated it to be about ninety feet by approximating the height of the hill above the entrance. It wasn't known if the floor of the cave was level, or whether it rose or fell as it penetrated the hill. They just had to hope their guess was close. If it weren't long enough, with any luck the remaining distance wouldn't be that much of a drop. It was a chance they had to take.

As they sat in a circle weaving the rope, Jacobs said, "Jabaar, I've been thinking about what you said the other day regarding the Muslim religion. I have always wondered why there *was* a war against Christianity in ancient times. Here's what I think. You say Islam teaches peace, yet what we see practiced is a religion based on *hate*...not *love*, like Christianity. And to me, the reason is simple: Jesus was a Jew. I think that's the reason this all started in the first place.

Worshipping a Jew is basically unacceptable to Arabs. They have hated the Jews for thousands of years. In my opinion Muhammad, an Arab, invented himself as a Prophet and superior successor to Jesus. He cleverly included Jesus in his teachings to give his new religion credibility; and used it to remind his followers that Christianity was based on Jewish origins to subtly create animosity between the two religions."

Jabaar shook his head. "I understand why you say Islam is based on hate. It was not always that way. The eleventh century Christian Crusade against Islam was cruel and vicious."

"But didn't the Crusade start because the Muslims had brutally conquered Jerusalem and Palestine earlier, and the Crusade was a response—a way to recapture the Holy Land?"

"That is correct. Blood is on the hands of both religions."

"Children are taught to hate in your schools, a negative infection at a very young age. If the same amount of time had been spent surrounded by love for one another, that goodness would have infected them as well, only positively. It's difficult to believe any God would put people into this world to purposely destroy it along with His human beings, whether they were believers or non-believers. As both were created by Him, I think Allah would be displeased."

Jacobs added, "Christianity and Islam are the two largest religions in the world. Christians still promote peace wherever they go and help wherever they can...like the victims of that huge tsunami disaster in Indonesia. It seems that Muslims are so intent on converting people that they don't take the time to care for them or provide them with hope.

"If people don't believe in Islam, why should a Muslim care, other than to feel sorry for them because they won't go to Paradise when they die? That is not a reason to kill. And yet, nasty people always seem to find reasons to be nasty. They say American society is decadent. I admit our society is more decadent today than it has been. But to kill everyone because of it, in my mind is a worse sin. And isn't the promise of seventy-two virgins for an eternity to a martyr who kills others decadent, as it relies on sex for fulfillment?"

Jabaar shrugged. "Nobody will ever know for sure. No religion is perfect for everyone. I think the Christian idea for peaceful coexistence is best for world. I support both religions, and hope my own country comes to its senses and does the same."

Owens, who had continued to watch the cave's entrance as he worked on the rope, interrupted the conversation. "Activity over there."

Johnson, assigned to watch the exhaust hole, was out of sight on the other side of the road, and watched as one of the terrorists emerged and started to climb the hill toward where he was stationed. Owens had anticipated this possibility, so Johnson was well hidden.

The man went directly to the hole, bent over and examined the exhaust hose, making sure it remained securely fastened so it wouldn't slip back down into the cave. Suddenly he looked around, apparently noticing something that wasn't quite right. He knelt for a closer look. Then he stood and, shading his eyes, inspected the surrounding terrain. He appeared to see nothing out of the ordinary, but was still not satisfied. Leaning over, he shouted down the hole, but there was no response.

Owens had no idea what he was saying. He turned to Jabaar. "What's he so excited about?"

"He has seen the heel print of a boot."

The terrorist hurried down the hill and raced back into the cave.

"Damn. That's all we need. Discovered because of a boot track? How are our shoes different than theirs?"

"They wear flat sandals. No boots."

"That mountain's all rock. How could there be any tracks up there?"

"Maybe dirt from the brush placed next to hole."

"Charlie's boot…when he examined the exhaust hose."

Johnson was now in sight, waving to the others. Once he got their attention, he held his arms out with his palms up, wondering what was happening.

Jacobs said, "They sweep their tracks to hide the location of the cave. We need to do the same around the hole. Charlie's the only one who can do it soon enough to help."

Owens pointed at his own boots and then to the ground. Jacobs brought over a tree branch and started sweeping the ground where Owens was pointing. It was like a game of charades, only the stakes were much higher. After a few seconds Johnson's face lit up and he gave them a thumbs up.

Owens pumped his arm, motioning for him to hurry. Johnson smoothed out the small patch of dirt, making sure not to raise any dust in the process. He then headed back toward his hiding place, but kept on going in case they decided to investigate the entire hillside.

Moments later the same terrorist appeared with another man, both armed. They hurried up the hill. Reaching the hole, the first terrorist stopped, again knelt, and then quickly rose, shaking his head. The heel print was gone. But it had been there just minutes ago... The other man lashed out at him.

Jabaar said, "He is very angry. He went up there for nothing. He said if it happens again, he would beat him worse than the prisoners. Does he understand? He answered, 'Yes Qa-'id.' That means leader."

"So that's the guy who started this. I'll be looking him up," Owens said.

The terrorists made their way back down the hill, the first man's head bowed in shame. They pushed back through the brush and disappeared into the cave.

Owens said, "We were lucky that time. We need to be more careful. We can't leave evidence like that around."

Johnson appeared, gave the high sign that everything was OK, and limped back to his post as a muffled scream could be heard from within the cave.

℟

Schick picked up the telephone after just one ring. "Superintendent's office." The caller identified himself and asked to speak to Randall, who had just walked in. "Boss, it's headquarters."

"I'll take it in my office." Randall closed the door behind him. This would be the second day in a row he had spoken to senior management about how they could help save the lives of his captured drivers. He had a feeling this conversation wouldn't be much different than the others.

"What do you mean we don't have any money to bail 'em out? We've got to come up with something, even if it's just a few million. Surely our company can do that! What about insurance? What about a bank loan?"

"Our policy doesn't cover this type of catastrophe. We contacted them first thing this morning. And we talked with our bank too. The only way a loan would be considered is for us to put up dollar-for-dollar collateral. We would be risking our entire company if we did that...something we aren't prepared to do."

The Chief Financial Officer added, "How much would it cost to replace the entire crew and how long would it take?"

"Replace? What are you talking about? We might not ever be able to replace them."

"Calm down, Randall...or do we need to send someone over there to handle this?"

"Not necessary. I just want to make sure you understand that once it's public knowledge these drivers were killed because our company refused to come up with the money, we could double the pay and still not get any takers."

"We understand that. But putting that aside for a minute, hypothetically what would be the hard-dollar cost involved to replace them?"

"Our headhunter charges us $30,000 per man. The signing bonus is also $30,000. The airfare averages $2,000, and there are other miscellaneous expenses. We're looking at roughly $65,000 each. We need to replace seventeen men at that camp, even though we still have four drivers unaccounted for. Total cost would be a little over one million dollars — if we can get them."

"One point one million dollars to be precise. Those are the hard-dollar recruiting costs. What else?"

"It doesn't include our daily revenue loss between now and the time we hire and train the replacements. Probably close to another million."

"So we could be looking at a couple of million dollars, right?"

"Yes. But again, that assumes we can find men who would *want* to drive for us after they learn about the last group."

"Yes, yes. As I said, we understand all that."

After an uncomfortable silence the CFO said, "Tom, our president is sitting next to me and has been listening in. He sympathizes with your situation and wants to do something to help. He has authorized us to offer the terrorists two million dollars.

33

"Two million when they're asking for thirteen? That will just piss 'em off more."

"It's all we can do, in spite of the fact that they have Murdock too. Murdock is…quite wealthy."

"Murdock is rich?"

"That's an understatement, but don't tell anyone. They might find out and ask for even more. Now, when you announce it on the Baghdad TV station as they demanded, explain that we have been losing money because of the high cost of doing business, and that the amount we are offering is all we can pull together on such short notice. Can you handle that?"

"Yes. But what happens if they take the two million and then tell us we have another few days to round up the rest? What do we say?"

"I'm afraid the answer will have to be it's all we can do. This is not a down payment…it *is* the payment! We'll have to suffer the consequences if it isn't enough."

Randall said, "Actually, it's our drivers who will suffer the consequences. We can make up the financial loss…but not bring back a life."

"Do the best you can. We don't have the money…it's just that simple."

"I'll try, but I live over here. I don't think it will be enough to buy their release." He paused a moment, then added, "May God have mercy on their souls…because we sure don't," and he hung up in disgust.

ℜ

"Get down. Sounds like that truck again."

The vehicle that had brought in supplies the day before was back, its bed full...just like the last time. Again, it stopped in front of the bushes. The driver, different from the last one, wore civilian clothes with a tattered tan shirt, his head wrapped in cloth. He looked around before saying, "Allah blesses you."

Owens scowled. "Damn. It's a different signal."

The foliage was pushed away and the truck quickly disappeared into the cave, its tire tracks swept clean. It happened fast. They doubtless expected their delivery at this time.

"A man must be stationed at the entrance. Minimizes the possibility of detection," Owens muttered.

Half an hour later the bushes parted and the driver returned the way he had come. As before, all that remained after the truck rounded the bend was the silence of the afternoon.

What had happened was important to the plan Owens had been considering. "Two days in a row. If we're lucky, the truck might come every day. This could be really good."

It helped him piece together his biggest question regarding reconnaissance within the cave before their rescue attempt. In spite of the different signal by the driver, now they could actually consider utilizing the truck. There were at least two different drivers, which was good. And he also surmised that they had contact with the outside world through the driver once a day—potentially more, if they had a transmitter.

Owens decided they had to immediately move forward with a plan to intercept the truck. It was critical to know what to expect inside the cave if they were to have any hope of freeing the hostages and surviving the attempt. They would need to stop the driver a mile or so before reaching the cave, take his clothes and substitute Jabaar. They would also need to learn that day's signal before eliminating the driver. That would be tricky.

The old guys were confident they could commandeer the truck, but could the young Iraqi fulfill his part? He appeared much too innocent looking. The terrorists, including the two drivers, were tough-looking men. Granted, Jabaar now had a stubble of a beard, as did all of them, and looked a bit more menacing than before. But his demeanor—and in particular his eyes—exposed him as an untested boy. He needed to develop a tougher look...fierce, ready to attack at a moment's notice. If he weren't convincing, they would be defeated before they'd even begun.

They had just started discussing this problem when Johnson, who had rejoined them shortly after the heel track incident, said, "Jabaar, come with me. We've got some work to do."

They moved away from the group, and Johnson told him, "OK, give me your fiercest look."

Jabaar stared at him with his normal, passive face.

"No, no, that's not it, that's how you always look. We've got to change it and quick."

"I will try."

"First, your posture. You stand with your head tilted down. This is submissive. These guys aren't subservient to anyone. Get that head up. Be defiant. Hold your chin out as if you are looking down on others, and don't slump. Pull your shoulders back and stick out your chest."

"You mean like you?"

"No, not your stomach like me...your chest."

Jabaar exaggerated everything suggested until he was bent over backwards.

"This very uncomfortable. Can't hold this position too long, but will try."

Johnson started laughing and Jabaar joined him, realizing how ridiculous he must have looked. Jabaar then straightened up and stood taller than before. He held his head high, his shoulders back and his chest out a bit more than before.

"Now you're starting to cook. That's a lot better. But you gotta remember to breathe."

Johnson had noticed Jabaar's face getting red. His color came back as he inhaled deeply, but his old posture returned.

"OK, now we need to put the two together. You need to look like a man, not a defeated boy. Try it."

Jabaar assumed a stronger posture and took a breath at the same time.

"That's great. Now then, when you talk, look the other person square in the eye. You got that?"

"Yes…look in eye. That will be difficult."

"Let's give it a shot. Look me in the eye."

Jabaar remained standing straighter, but his same soft eyes defeated the image.

"Still not there yet. Let's try something. Imagine you are six feet tall. Then, imagine how you would feel if you were trained in judo and karate. You're capable of breaking the neck of a man twice your size if someone messes with you. Now, imagine that a man hits your mother, knocking her to the ground. You're standing only a few feet away. Look at me the way you would look at that man before nailing him."

Jabaar looked at Johnson again, this time with not only hatred in his eyes but with nostrils flared and a sneer on his lips. He stood even taller, chest pumped up, and ready to lash out.

Johnson grinned. "Easy, big guy. That's it. That's the look you need. It even scared me. We'll work on this several times a day. Who knows, after we're done here you might wind up liking your new image. Go back to your village and kick some ass if somebody pisses you off. Now then, about your voice…"

ℜ

The time had come for them to prepare themselves physically for the upcoming rescue attempt. This meant that everyone, even Jabaar, needed to be in shape. One or two of them—it hadn't yet been determined who—would need to be able to climb down into the cave without being heard. This would require strength and endurance. Owens was in the best shape of them all, even though he was the oldest. Serving as a drill instructor in charge of physical training at Camp Pendleton, along with working as a physical fitness instructor at a gym in Southern California, hadn't hurt.

Owens had started them on a physical fitness program the first week he arrived at Camp Mojave so they could better perform their everyday tasks, which included a certain amount of lifting—unlike the same job in the States. They started out in poor shape, but improved immensely under his tutelage. Knowing which muscles would be needed to perform this new task effectively, he focused on these areas.

In so short a time they couldn't be made much stronger than they already were. But they could tone up what they had. Owens wanted to attack soon to save as many lives as possible, but knew that was impractical. He figured it would take many days to make enough rope and gather the necessary intel to execute a workable plan. For now, all he wanted to accomplish with his men was to make each a little steadier, and strong enough to not fall when scaling down the hole. The amount of time it would take to get to the bottom shouldn't be more than a minute or so. That's how long they would have to be able to hold onto the rope without letting go.

They began by exercising their arms, chest and shoulders, first warming up by slowly running in place before stretching. Their actual strength exercises started with push-ups, then pull-ups on a nearby tree. To help their coordination and hand strength, they tossed heavy rocks to one another over short distances. When they first picked up the rocks, they bent over using only their arms to lift.

Owens corrected them. "I know in the past I mentioned the importance of working your smaller muscles, but when lifting, you need to use your larger muscles whenever possible. Use your legs to pick up these rocks to minimize the strain on your back. Small muscles should only be used when appropriate. This advice applies to a lot of situations. In fact, throughout history, many a man has gotten into unnecessary trouble because he used his *small* muscle when common sense, if he listened to it, told him not to. You can read into that whatever you want."

Everyone chuckled at Owens's historical observation. They worked out for another hour, including squats and running up and down the hill for endurance. Numley and Johnson struggled the most, and started to speed up the exercises to get them over with quicker.

Owens corrected that too. "You've got to slow down to get the best results in the shortest period of time. And you have to go slow when you're going with gravity. This is when you get the greatest gain and muscle build."

All of them ached in muscles they didn't even know existed. This routine was far more strenuous compared to what they had been doing back at camp. Numley appeared to be in the most pain, and his complaints were the loudest.

"I can't do this. I'm strong enough. I can make it down that hole if I have to. I've got to rest now."

"You can rest when you're dead."

"You don't get it. I'm done with this bullshit."

Owens glared at him. "You're done when I say you're done."

"Screw you! Go harass somebody else for a change. I'm through for today."

Numley may have saved the day earlier by finding the first food, but everyone grew tired of his complaints. Jacobs occasionally referred to him as Rodney Numb Nuts, as he always seemed to be out of sync with the rest of the group.

Owens picked Numley up by his shirt collar and got in his face. "You're the weakest of the bunch. You bitch the most and do the least. You'll be the one to screw up when it counts, and I don't want my life or any of theirs depending on you."

As he let go of him he added, "Now hit it so you'll be ready."

"Who made you the boss anyway?"

Owens glared at him. "If somebody else wants to take over, do it—but do it now."

Johnson said, "No thanks Dave. I trust you. I think all of us do. I'm tired too, but you know better'n us what needs to be done. I'll give it my all."

Johnson, though in the poorest shape, never complained. As a result, he had gained respect from the others, except Numley.

Jacobs quipped, "Yeah Dave, you are the man. But let me remind you that as a Marine, you were just a department of the Navy. I was an officer in the Navy and we wrote your paychecks."

"We're a department of the Navy all right. The *Men's* Department!"

Everyone laughed. The tension created by Numley had been broken. Owens knew that humor almost always lessened tension, and he was pleased that Jacobs had set it up. They were coming together as a team and growing in character in spite of the adversity. After this, they completed another series of exercises. They knew in the long run that these efforts just might save their lives.

ℜ

Pissed? An understatement. Randall was enraged. He kept running through the last conversation with corporate. No help whatsoever. Based on what the terrorists had said, at most the two million would only buy two lives. He wouldn't even be given the chance to decide which two would be saved...not that he would want to make that type of decision.

When he learned that Murdock was loaded, Randall immediately tracked down his people stateside. He needed another eleven million and this was his only hope. They were, of course, shocked to learn their boss was one of the thirteen men taken prisoner by the terrorists. The names of the hostages had not been disclosed due in large part to the four missing drivers. Nobody knew for sure who had been captured and who had escaped — or died in the desert trying.

"But even if we give them the money, what assurance do we have that his life will be spared?" Murdock's business manager, still in shock, attempted to cover all the angles, but there was no doubt he would try to come up with the required funds.

"You're asking if we can trust these people, and your guess is as good as mine."

"So we're all operating on hope then." The line was quiet for a few seconds and then he continued: "I think we can get the money together in one or two days at most. But don't promise anything until we do. Under the best of circumstances, the soonest we can get it to Baghdad will be Friday morning. The question is, how do we get it to the terrorists by *their* deadline?"

"Right now, I don't know. But I'll find a way. Just get that money over here…and thank you. I'll call with a plan as soon as I have one."

ℜ

Pride, dignity, and maybe even revenge, now drove the old guys. The ordeal had turned personal. They had to succeed. And to succeed, they needed to be willing to do whatever it took. They may not actually have to *do* everything, just be willing. The terrorists had captured and killed too many other Americans. They couldn't be allowed to get away with this atrocity as well.

In addition to the exercises, Owens had other training for them as well. "Gather 'round everybody, I want to make sure you understand the mechanics of an assault rifle."

He held up Jabaar's weapon, an M16-A1, and described it in detail. The clip had thirty rounds of ammunition. That was *all* they had to get the job done. Thirty rounds. It would need to be used sparingly. The safety was found on the right side. To fire the rifle, it needed to be released by pressing forward with the right thumb. When not in use, the safety was pulled back to lock it.

"The terrorists are using AK-47's, at least that's what it sounded like when they attacked our camp."

He told them the Russians probably supplied their guns, as that was where they were manufactured, and that they were going to need to get one or two of them early in the attack to turn the odds in their favor. Owens explained that they were assault rifles too, but with some variation. Their ammunition was slightly larger in caliber compared to the M16 and their overall length was about 100 millimeters shorter, but it still weighed more. Its rate of fire was also a bit slower, but that difference was immaterial. The safety on that rifle, was in the same location as the M16, and was released in the same manner.

"Remember, the rifle will not fire if the safety is on. When you get your hands on one, the first thing you want to do is to make sure the safety is off so you can use it. Understood?"

Numley said, "Got it. Release the safety right away so it will shoot when needed. I will *not* forget that rule."

"I've been doing a lot of thinking about this mission, and here's one of our biggest problems. This is our only weapon, and I'm the only one, other than Jabaar, who has ever fired this type of rifle. So, I will need to lead the attack with it, coming in from the front. Keith, you and Rodney will need to climb down the rope and come in the back way, as we have already discussed. Draw straws to decide who goes first. We'll assume fifteen minutes for the two of you to get down the rope and be in position to attack, as we won't be able to signal each other. While you're doing that, Jabaar will bring up the supply truck we commandeer so we can get out of here with the others as fast as possible. Charlie, I haven't forgotten about you, but as hard as you're working, I don't see you climbing down that hole. Any problem with that?"

"Nope! None at all."

"You'll come in the entrance with me. But, you'll still need to be in good shape to be effective."

Johnson's smile immediately left his face as he had wrongly thought his workouts had ended.

"The objective will be for the two of you to find a weapon as soon as possible. It'll be dark, and we don't have any night goggles, so it will be difficult. Our only chance is the element of surprise. They should be spread around— that's how I would deploy them—but for all we know they could be grouped together. We won't know until the attack. You'll have to be creative once you're inside the cave. We'll practice several different strategies before you go in. Assuming one or both of you can get your hands on a rifle, the very first thing you will need to do is...?"

Jacobs said, "Make sure the safety is off so it's instantly operable."

"That's right. Now, you need to know what to expect when you pull the trigger. All rifles have a kick to them and also have a tendency to jerk upward slightly when fired. So if you're not thinking and you hold the rifle too loosely, you could wind up shooting over their heads. Not a good tactic and a waste of bullets. Keith, show me how you think a rifle should be held."

Jacobs brought the rifle up to his shoulder in what he thought was the right firing position.

Owens said, "Almost...but not quite. First of all, you need to press the butt of the rifle firmly against your shoulder so that it becomes almost like a second arm. This will minimize its kick when you fire it and also improve your aim. Once you are holding it tight enough, lay your cheek alongside it to sight your longer shots. You probably won't have time for this when you're reacting quickly in the cave to save your ass, but if you need to take a longer shot, remembering to do this might even help you hit your target."

"That would be good," Numley said.

"I want all of you to practice holding this rifle so you can get comfortable with it. You'll need that comfort when working under the pressure you're going to experience in the cave. The bullets come out fast, something like 600 rounds per minute. Just like our rifle, you will only have thirty rounds, assuming you have a full clip, so use them sparingly. You can run out of ammunition in a matter of seconds, so you will need to lightly squeeze and quickly release the trigger. But before you do that, you must aim it! Every bullet fired without hitting somebody is a bullet wasted. Even more important, I will be coming in from the front. If you miss one of them, that bullet might hit me. So you will have to think with every shot you take. Am I making myself clear?"

"Yes sir, Sarge," they replied in unison.

ℜ

Water, food and a place to sleep. The necessities of life were taken care of. But, there was so much more to do. The exercises were exhausting, and they had only been at it for one day. When they dropped from fatigue, they worked on the rope. That wasn't easy either. Digging up tree roots took effort, then they had to be cleaned and carefully braided. It all seemed impossible. Jacobs had gone for water, as they were on their last bottle.

Numley mused, "Could things get any worse?"

That's when the sandstorm began. They had all experienced sandstorms as one came along every other week or so, some lasting longer than others.

Numley said, "You know, I was hoping to already be in the cave, or in the truck, or maybe even back in Baghdad. Anywhere but out here. What do we do now?"

Early on, Owens had made the decision not to build a shelter for fear the terrorists might discover it. The fact that they were now confronted with this disastrous event found them unprepared. The winds reached speeds in excess of one hundred miles per hour, with some clocked at a hundred and forty five. It would approximate a category four hurricane if coming in from the ocean. The force of the sand at this speed could literally peel the skin off a man in minutes. They had all heard horrible stories about people trapped in a sandstorm with no place to hide.

All of them crouched down as low as possible, using nearby scrub brush for protection.

As the storm quickly increased in intensity, day turned into night. The sun cast a deep orange-red glow as the windswept sand rose between it and the ground. Eventually it grew so thick that sunlight was blocked out completely as the sand wrought havoc on everything in its path.

Powerful, dry winds blowing across the desert were the cause of most sandstorms, the intense desert heat creating the strong convection currents that trigger them. The combination of heat and an approaching cold front produced the tornado-like conditions. The leading edge of sandstorms, which often can reach a mile into the sky, appear as a high wall of dust. It got into everything, and it could make a firearm inoperable, clogging the moving parts, which would then require extensive cleaning for it to work again. Sandstorms seemed to come out of nowhere and there was never any advance warning.

Owens shouted to Jabaar, "Put something around your rifle to protect it!"

Jabaar quickly wrapped it in a rag and then told the others, "Follow me and bring digging tools."

"What do we do about Keith? He's all alone out there," Johnson said.

"He's on his own. Right now it's every man for himself."

Jabaar verified the main direction of the wind with its swirling mass of silt, dust and sand, a difficult task, as it always seemed to come from all directions, and led them to the opposite side of the hill.

ℜ

Jacobs couldn't believe it. He had just finished filling up the bottles when the sand started to race through the ravine, engulfing him with its dark, choking and deadly fury. He was a long way from the others. Should he try to get back to them, or what? What could…*should* he do to stay alive? It was already too dark to look for any shelter. He needed to make a decision, and make it fast, or he would be past tense when the storm was over.

ℜ

By the time Jabaar found an acceptable location, visibility was almost zero. The blinding sand penetrated their skin with its needle-like force.

He shouted, "Find a soft place, dig hole, then lie in it with back to wind. You will be covered with sand, but that OK. It will help protect you from cutting blast until winds die down."

The holes became a reality in record time, no doubt due to the adrenalin that pumped through their bodies. They clambered into their hand-made holes, covering their heads with their jackets for additional protection from the sting of the biting sand.

Stifling and gagging, with a dry dusty smell that would never be forgotten, sand was everywhere. At least it wasn't cutting into their skin anymore. Jabaar was right: the little man-made holes really did protect them from the most painful part of the storm.

Breathing, however, was a different story, even with the protection of their jackets. A full breath was impossible. Fine silt mingled with sand, making them gag and forcing them to take short breaths so as not to suck it too deeply into their lungs. This was the sickening feeling of suffocation.

Johnson shouted to the sky, "Lord, please make this here storm a short one."

ℜ

Ali and the informant huddled in a corner discussing their next steps. "Still no word from the infidel Americans. Maybe they are foolish enough to taunt us with silence and think we will do nothing?"

The informant replied, "We both know it has always been their policy not to negotiate for captives. It's the trucking company that needs to respond to our demands."

"If we had more money like other al-Qa'ida cells, they wouldn't even be given this opportunity for us to spare their people. They would already be dead."

This small group of operatives lacked money because they had spent everything provided them when they first formed their cell. The al-Qa'ida was established by Osama bin Ladin in 1988 to bring together Arabs who had fought in Afghanistan against the Soviet invasion. The goal was to continue the Jihad in other countries. It developed into a multi-national support group that funded and orchestrated the activities of Islamic militants around the world, initially using the $300 million bin Ladin had inherited from his billionaire father, then incorporating donations regularly received from like-minded supporters as well as money illegally siphoned from Muslim charitable organizations. All efforts were aimed at overthrowing what it saw as the corrupt and heretical governments of Muslim states, replacing them with the rule of Sharia (Islamic law).

The United States is considered the main enemy of Islam, which is why al-Qa'ida is so anti-Western. Bin Ladin has been quoted as saying, "If someone can kill an American soldier, it is better than wasting time on other matters." As history has demonstrated, his minions have gone well beyond the killing of American soldiers, focusing their activities on innocent civilians from all countries, including Muslims throughout the Middle East.

Ali continued: "As you know, before joining forces with Sahir Umar in Iran, we had to steal our food just to exist. If the trucking company doesn't reply in time, the consequences will be disastrous for them. Our demands *will* be honored so we can continue our work here. We will not be stopped by a lack of money, not when we are so close to victory."

The informant nodded. "They know the deadline. If they are smart, they are trying to get the money to us right now."

Ali replied in frustration, "While we wait, I will continue to enjoy beating more of them myself. I want them to never forget us, and what we stand for. If they survive, maybe it will convince them to get out of Iraq and stay out. Any hesitation in delivering the money will result in death. I will personally kill the first one myself, sending the American infidels a strong message that we mean business."

℞

The three old guys and their Iraqi guard fell into a deep sleep almost immediately, exhausted from exercise that now included the digging of these new holes. When they awoke several hours later, the sandstorm had subsided to a point that the sun had regained much of its normal white-hot luster. They had survived another disaster and were grateful to be alive.

Numley muttered as they shook the sand from their clothing, "I'll never ask if it can get any worse. Out here it can *always* get worse."

"Now we've got to find Keith." Owens was up and had already started moving toward the ravine, taking Jabaar with him. "I hope to hell he made it."

ℜ

"Keith. Are you still down here?"

Owens and Jabaar stood at the water hole in the ravine. Along the way they had quietly called out in hopes he would hear them. Nowhere to be found, the filled water bottles laying next to the water hole were the only evidence he had been there.

"Where would he have gone?"

Jabaar looked around and pointed up the ravine. "The sand entered from that direction. He probably go this way, even if only to keep his back to the sand."

The two headed down into the ravine, hoping that Jacobs had found a protected spot that would save him from the cutting blast of the sand. There were no tracks to follow. The wind and sand had taken care of that.

They traveled deeper into the ravine, farther than any of them had gone before.

"I don't think he could go this far, not with all the sand blinding him—."

"Wait, did you hear that?" Owens had abruptly stopped.

"Help. Help," could be faintly heard somewhere nearby.

"Where's that coming from? I don't see him."

Jabaar knelt at the edge of a large rock where they had stopped and looked down into a deep crevice. Jacobs hung upside down, securely held by one leg caught in a root that protruded near the top of the rock. He had not fallen far, but had been unable to free himself from the grasp of the root.

Although uncomfortable, the location had protected him from the sand as it flew past him safely overhead.

Owens said, "Don't move. We'll get you out of there."

He reached down and took hold of his leg. "Raise up and grab my arm. Jabaar will cut the root so we can pull you up."

Jacobs attempted to comply, but only got halfway up before groaning and falling back to the same position.

"I can't do it. I've been hanging here too long. I don't have any strength left."

"The hell you say. You don't have a choice. Just do it."

He struggled again, groaning, then screaming as he slowly raised up close enough to grab Owens' outstretched arm.

"OK. I did it. Now be careful. It's a long way down."

"Don't worry. You're not going anywhere. We've still got a lot of work for you to do."

ℜ

As they ate some more of their meager rations, pride starting to build up in each as they had completed another successful day, Numley looked over at Jabaar and said, "What's your story? How did you wind up guarding a bunch of truck drivers anyway?"

Jabaar looked up, surprised by the attention. He had felt like he was just a fixture, someone who was only there when needed. He collected his thoughts before responding.

"My family is very poor. We live in Baghdad, the Sunni Triangle, and still see violence every day, although not as bad as it used to be.

"We used to see neighbors beaten, even killed by the Hussein Republican Guard, killing three deep if they suspected treason."

"Three deep? What does that mean?" Jacobs asked.

"It means killing three family members, usually father and two children. Hussein guards drag whole family into street. They want everyone to see. First they torture two children, then kill them. Then, they torture father, but let him live for short time in agony before killing him. The bodies are dumped in the desert. American soldiers already find three hundred gravesites, the smallest with two thousand bodies. Hussein killed millions just to make sure he stayed in power.

"My uncle was one of them. Aunt and cousins now live with us. This is why I needed to work. We are poor already. I earn money so family not starve."

Owens and Jacobs looked at each other and bowed their heads, empathetic toward the plight of Jabaar and his family.

"When we hear the United States was going to attack Iraq to get Hussein, we think, good! Anything is better than him, and I still think so, in spite of all the killings today. They are less than they were under Hussein. Many towns already have democracy. Mayors get elected and rebuild without soldiers. This is what we want in our area."

Numley said, "We came over here because of weapons of mass destruction. That turned out to be bogus. That's why I'm so against this war."

Jabaar said, "We had them. And according to Alaa Al-Tamimi, a director general in the Iraq nuclear program, our country came within a month of producing an atomic bomb. If Hussein had not invaded Kuwait, provoking the first war with United States, he would have the bomb. The embargo stopped him. And everyone knows he used chemicals on our own people.

"To win here, you need to win the hearts and minds of the people. I see your soldiers doing that. Terrorists aren't doing it. That's why I think you will achieve your goal...then your troops can go home.

"I don't have a wife like Charlie did, but there is a girl I like. She is beautiful, but comes from wealth. It would be an insult to her family if I approached her. She does not know I like her, or even exist, I think. My father did some work at her house. I saw her when I helped him. Now I must do something to earn her love. I need to prove myself worthy."

Johnson said, "Maybe you're doing it right now, partner."

"Maybe. I became a guard to earn money to help family...but also to help country. I thought first about joining new army, but best Iraqi soldiers get killed. I think terrorists notice them, know they could be dangerous, so eliminate. Truck driver guard also sounded important, but maybe not so dangerous as army. Pay is better, but I was wrong. It turned out dangerous too.

"I am never in fight, never hurt anyone. I don't *want* to hurt anyone, but have no choice now. That's why I'm still here, and not run away. I know you wondered if I would stay. I see it in your eyes. This is *my* country. I know how to survive in it. I could leave at any time...go home. But I have run all my life and am tired of it."

Owens got up, walked over to Jabaar and sat down next to him, putting his arm around his shoulders. "We appreciate you staying by our side, and if weren't for you, we might not even be alive right now. Thank you for that. You'll do great and we'll get through this together as a team."

Jacobs added, "That goes for me too. We're all here because of problems...at home *and* over here. Now, instead of problems from a cruel dictator, they're from infiltrators from other countries, killing far more innocent Iraqis than American troops. Some think they are just insurgents, internal discontent, and there is a lot of that between the Sunnis and Shi'ites, but much of the murderous activities are by people from outside the country—terrorists, not insurgents."

Owens added, "And many of the suicide bombers have been forced by the terrorists to blow themselves up to save their families. It's a myth that everyone wants to become a martyr in order to go to Paradise and enjoy lots of virgins for eternity."

"Iraqis show a lot of courage when they vote," Jacobs said, "with over half of their population showing up at the polls in spite of the death threats. Now they need the courage to take those same blue fingers they got when they voted and use them to point out the terrorists killing so many of their own people. If they'd do it, this country would win their own war against terrorism. Then *our* troops could go home. I think Jabaar is a great example of the good that's happening over here."

Jabaar nodded. "I like that blue finger idea. Our people want to help save our country. Most of us are still afraid. I'm not brave, but am trying. I voted. Others try too. Most all of us thank you for what you are doing."

Numley raised a hand. "Not to change the subject, but I have a question about our plan. Assuming we kill these terrorists and rescue the guys, what do you think will happen to us when we get back to the States? I remember when our soldiers came back from Vietnam; there were folks that spit on them, like ole Jane what's-her-face and some of her political friends. Do you think that could happen to us?"

Owens, enraged, said, "Spitting on soldiers was the least of what that bitch did as she protested the war. She actually went to North Vietnam and became a propaganda tool for their government. She even posed for pictures with the enemy, including one where she sat on the gunner's seat of an anti-aircraft gun with an enemy helmet on her head, surrounded by grinning North Vietnamese soldiers. She also voluntarily made broadcasts on Radio Hanoi, calling

American pilots war criminals—urging them to stop the bombing. She said she knew first-hand that North Vietnam was treating their captives humanely, solely based on discussions with prisoners that were coerced by their captors. When POWs returned home in 1973 telling of their torture, Jane said they were lying if they assert it was North Vietnamese policy to torture American prisoners. She was nicknamed Hanoi Jane by our troops, and should have been jailed for treason. She was just another loud-mouthed *enlightened* entertainer with her head up her ass—just like so many of them today. I won't go to any of their movies. I've shed real blood for this country, and the only thing most of them have done is act—act out real life instead of actually living life in the trenches. I won't support them with my money."

"I don't know about the rest of you," Johnson said, "but I sure hope that woman tries the same thing with us, and that she gets close enough to spit on me. I'll have a big surprise for her."

He spat a big wad of tobacco juice on a nearby rock, where it slithered down its face in a dark and disgusting manner.

"Yep, I sure do hope she gets close to me!"

He chuckled over that for quite a while before finally falling asleep.

Day Six – Thursday, January 12th

"IME TO WORK OUT again, guys. It'll help save our lives."

Owens knew everyone was tired, but also knew that determination could overcome exhaustion.

"If you need an incentive, think about the men inside the cave and what they must be going through. Compared to that, we've got it soft."

They had to be strong enough when they dropped down into the cave, not only to save the other men, but also to stay alive doing it.

"We've got to get in, then get out...fast! They may have something that will help us get home, but we won't know until we're in there."

Numley stood and glared at Owens. "This whole thing sucks. Who do we think we are anyway? Warriors? Well, we aren't."

"You already down for the count, Numley? Not even willing to try?"

"This is going to get us killed—*all* of us."

"What's the alternative? Die trying to get home with your tail between your legs?"

"Don't pull that crap on me. At least, with that option, there's a chance. I don't see any hope with what you're suggesting."

"When you're on offense, there's always hope. Some of our greatest generals had doubts about military missions. General Patton told his troops, '*When in doubt, attack.*' It kept the enemy off balance and was a major reason for his success."

"He led an *army*. We're not the army! We're a bunch of civilians."

"I know that. But you're even better. For this mission you're a Marine — led and trained by a Marine. And when you go home — and you will — it will be with your head held high."

Numley sat down, not necessarily convinced, just overpowered for the time being.

Jacobs asked, "Dave, what about this rope? We aren't making much headway. Are there any other options?"

"Well, I originally considered two others, but both are far more dangerous."

Numley jumped at a second chance to voice his displeasure. "What are they? Maybe *we* should be the judge."

Owens scowled at him. "Have you heard the expression, 'break a leg,' when a performer goes on stage? The other way is to inch yourself down that hole with your back pressed on one side and your legs pressed against the other. Two problems: you could knock dirt and rocks loose going down, letting 'em know that you're on the way. And when you get to the bottom — you know, the cave's roof — you'll be in a freefall until you hit the floor. That's when you could actually break your leg."

"That one doesn't make much sense."

"We could just attack through the front entrance. But, with only one weapon, we wouldn't get many of 'em before they started shooting back. We'd be sitting ducks."

"So, we really don't have a choice. We've got to finish this damn rope, don't we?"

"I'm afraid so."

Since yesterday's sandstorm, Owens had grown concerned about the limitations of their plan. Another storm could strike at any time. They needed an escape plan that would work whether there was a sandstorm or not. The way it looked now, many of them would have to walk to Numley's truck; the small supply vehicle wasn't large enough to carry all of them in one trip. Johnson would then have to try to fix that truck in the dark before they could drive it a short fifty or sixty miles until it ran out of gas, forcing them back on foot again. If that weren't enough, the condition of the men in the cave could not be all that good. Would any of them even be *able* to walk?

"Charlie, have you given any more thought to why Numley's truck stopped back there?" Owens asked.

"I still think it's electrical. But even then, it shouldn't have completely stopped like it did. I'd have to check it over to know for sure."

"How long would *that* take?"

"I could probably do it all in an hour."

"What's stopping you?" Owens grinned at Johnson and continued. "We need that truck to get everyone out of here fast. We can use whatever gas is left in the generator and the supply truck. Hopefully it'll be enough for a couple of hundred miles or so. I need you to walk back there, get it running and drive it back here. You'll need to hide it again and walk the rest of the way. I know it'll be tough on your leg. Do you think you can do it?"

Johnson shrugged. "Piece of cake."

He started off, energized, knowing he was about to play a major role in the success of their mission. He knew that if he failed, their mission would also most likely fail. He wasn't about to let that happen.

ℜ

Johnson reached the truck in under two hours. He'd slowed down en route, his limp more pronounced the longer he walked. He located the concealed truck and patted its front fender. "OK old girl. Time to get back to work."

Before lifting the hood, he looked under the front seat for anything that might be of use and found a pair of work gloves. "These will be a welcome sight for the boys climbing down the hole." He wondered why Numley hadn't mentioned them. "Probably forgot they were there."

He raised the hood to troubleshoot the problem. The truck was a fifteen-year-old Ford with an eight-cylinder, 370 horsepower gasoline engine. Johnson stood on his tiptoes, reaching over the fender of the front left wheel to examine the engine. As he began inspecting the lower electrical wires he heard a noise in the brush. He turned just in time to see a wild boar charge toward him. He immediately jumped onto the fender—no small feat for a man of his stature with bum legs—as the boar crashed into the tire where he had just stood. Stunned, the creature looked up and snorted, exposing its yellow fang-like teeth.

Johnson's body shook. He knew he had almost become this creature's breakfast. They would eat almost anything—including him, if given the chance.

Where had it come from? They had been outside for many days, and other than the wild dog and an occasional bird, they hadn't seen anything like this. Were there others? Autumn, their mating season, was when both males and females ran in groups called sounders. There could be anywhere from twenty to fifty of them.

Johnson looked around. Nothing. This one must have strayed from the herd. A relief, but what could he do? He couldn't fix the truck with that thing standing down there. He had to get rid of it.

The problem escalated. The boar rose up on its hind legs with the front ones balancing it on the tire and attempted to snare Johnson with its mouth—getting closer to one leg as it gnashed its teeth.

He now knew real fear. This animal wasn't going to give up. Johnson raised his wrench. He couldn't lean over too far for fear of falling. His first swing missed, as did the second. The third, however, grazed its head, the impact causing him to lose his grip. The wrench fell to the ground. Worse, the glancing blow seemed to make the boar even angrier as it continued snapping at his leg.

Johnson's only thought now was of survival. He grabbed his Phillips-head screwdriver, holding it like a dagger. The next time the animal leaped, he swung down hard, ramming the screwdriver deep into its right eye. The animal screeched and fell to the ground in pain, taking the screwdriver and Johnson with it. Blind in the one eye, bleeding profusely, it writhed in the dirt. Johnson extracted the screwdriver and plunged it first into the boar's neck, then its gut, yanking upward to tear at its internal organs.

The injured animal lashed out with its cloven hoof, hitting Johnson's shoulder. Ducking away from the flailing legs, he picked up a large rock, raised it high overhead, and brought it down on the boar's head. The animal continued to flail. *Was this damn thing ever going to die?* He brought the rock down again, this time from an even greater height, crushing its skull. The boar's legs shuddered, then were still.

Johnson lay next to the dead animal, his chest heaving as he sucked in air. Then, he laughed. "I guess I'm the one bringing home the bacon tonight!"

He stood and wiped the sweat off his face with a shirtsleeve, looking around to make sure there weren't any more of them. Then, he went back to work on the engine, standing on the front bumper instead of the ground. Within minutes he found what he was looking for.

As suspected, the rubber insulation had worn spots on several of the old spark plug wires leading from the distributor. The bare wires had bounced around on the chassis, grounding out each time they hit metal. That was the reason for the sputtering, but it shouldn't have stopped completely. He decided to wrap each wire with duct tape as a temporary fix before looking further. He didn't want any bare spots touching metal during their escape.

As he wrapped the last wire he saw the main problem. Spark plug wires grounding out was bad enough. But when the insulation on the primary wire from the coil to the distributor gets burned off because it was too long and laid against the hot exhaust manifold, it could shut down an engine. It would have to be insulated as well, but he decided to shorten it first so it wouldn't happen again. The heat from the exhaust manifold could melt duct tape in a matter of miles. When they got back, he would have a few words with the mechanics. They had taken the easy way out, attaching the wire to the side with a clip, which had come loose.

Half an hour later Johnson closed the hood and climbed into the cab. He turned the key to "on," pumped the accelerator pedal a couple of times to open the carburetor and pushed the starter button. The big engine turned over, a good sign that the battery was still strong. But it didn't start. He pressed the gas pedal several more times and turned the engine over again—nothing. He pushed even harder on the gas pedal and tried again. Same result.

He sat there bewildered, not knowing what to do next. He had to find a solution. This truck was the only way they could get everyone back to Baghdad. By his reckoning he had fixed everything that needed fixing to start the damn thing.

Johnson got out to look under the hood again, just in case he had missed something. That was when the first smell of smoke hit his nostrils from flames that poured out beneath the engine compartment.

"What the hell..."

Only then did he realize he might not only fail the others, but if the truck exploded, he might not even live to tell them about it.

ℜ

With the beatings beginning on Monday, the prisoners had suffered through three days of terror. Each had been forced to strip naked before being tied to the beating post. The captors had pointed at each penis and laughed, making jokes about their inadequate size. The goal? Humiliation...until total submission.

When a prisoner ultimately gave in to the demands of the captors, he was clothed and placed in the forward cell with an extra portion of bread and water as a reward. If a prisoner did not succumb, he was thrown back into the rear cell— naked, cold and trembling from the beating.

Two of Ali's henchmen pulled Murdock from the cage...again. He remained naked and sore from his punishment two days earlier. They forced him to his knees— the standard worshipping position voluntarily taken when one prays to God—but in this case he bowed before his captors, yet another way to humble a prisoner. His hands were tied to the beating post, leaving him unable to protect himself from what would ensue.

Ali stepped forward to administer the beating. He grabbed Murdock by the hair, pulling his head back with his face up so he could look him in the eye as he spoke. "Evidently we weren't forceful enough the first time. I will make sure we don't make that mistake again."

He glared at Murdock. "You say you are a consultant. What can you add to information gladly given to us by the others? Why are you in our country spying on us?"

Murdock said, "I just arrived. I haven't been here long enough to learn much of anything. My only job was to ride with the drivers, take notes and report my findings with recommendations to management. That's it. I am not a spy."

"You just got here? How many days ago?"

"One day."

Ali looked at the informant, who shook his head, indicating the statement was not true.

"You lie. You've been here spying on us longer than that!"

"How would you know how long I've been —?"

Murdock didn't finish his statement. A gloved fist pounded into his face, followed by a second and third blow.

"I don't believe you." Ali turned to his men. "Do you believe him?"

They cried, "No!" He hit him again. Blood gushed from his nose, and then from around his eyes.

"I will beat you until you admit your guilt."

Before Ali could land another blow, one of his men, caught up in the excitement, struck Murdock hard in the side of the head. He slumped forward, unconscious.

"You fool, I wanted to break him!" Ali shouted.

They splashed water in his face. He remained motionless. "Take him back to his cell."

Before they could comply, Ali looked in Murdock's face for a moment and then laughed. "As I thought...he's not breathing."

He turned and faced the rear cage. "Maybe this will convince the rest of you to talk when it is your turn."

ℜ

Gasoline. The fire was fueled by gasoline, a situation even worse than Johnson had first thought. The only way this fire could have begun was when he attempted to start the truck.

He quickly raised the hood, standing on the front bumper again, away from the flames, and examined the fuel pump connections. He immediately spotted the problem—a loose fuel line.

Johnson surmised that as the engine turned over the mechanical fuel pump, driven by the camshaft, had spewed gasoline over the dry foliage below. The mechanic that last worked on the truck must have forgotten to finish tightening the nut that connected the fuel line from the pump to the carburetor.

On his last attempt to start the truck, a spark from the battery cable at its connection point to the starter motor ignited the fumes that led back to its source: the gas-drenched weeds below. That was the only answer. If not extinguished quickly, it would cause an explosion that would destroy the truck — and Johnson with it.

"Shit. I started this thing. Think, damn it!"

Johnson knew he had to get the truck out of there or it would be totaled. He reached as far down as he could, locating the fuel pump underneath the engine and quickly re-attached the fuel line. He tightened the nut as firmly as he could before applying the wrench to finish the job. Flames licked up around his hands, forcing him to continually raise them up above the heat before plunging them down again until the task was completed. Only after he was done did he realize the job would have been less painful had he remembered to put on the work gloves he had just found. In spite of this, he tightened the nut in a matter of seconds. He hoped that this was the last problem.

He didn't even bother closing the hood as he swiftly climbed back behind the wheel to try again. If it didn't work this time, he would be a dead man. He swallowed hard, pushed the gas pedal down firmly, and again pressed the starter button. This time the engine caught hold. The old truck was back in business.

He slammed it into reverse and popped the clutch. The truck lurched backward, away from the blaze. Only then did he breathe easier. He had saved it, and himself, for the mission. But it wasn't over yet. The fire still needed to be put out so it wouldn't spread. He searched underneath the seat for the fire extinguisher that was supposed to be there. Nothing.

"Well," he muttered, "I don't have much of a choice now."

He jumped out of the truck and dove on top of the blaze, rolling back and forth in an effort to smother it with his bulk while it was still small. It worked. And other than a few minor burns on his hands, he had escaped unscathed.

He brushed himself off, thinking, *I'm getting too old for this shit.*

With the fire out, he dragged the dead boar to the road and, with all the strength he could muster, hefted it onto the lift at the back of the truck for loading.

Backing the truck away from the fire, he had crushed the bushes that had hidden it. He retrieved them from underneath the truck, fluffed them up, and placed them alongside the road. Lame, but maybe no one would notice. He climbed back into the truck and headed back toward the cave.

Thirty minutes later, Johnson was close enough to look for another place to hide the truck. He had to make sure it was well out of sight. This vehicle was their ticket to freedom.

ℜ

Two terrorists carried Murdock back to the cage and threw him in, locking the door behind him. The four men still remaining in the rear cage quickly gathered around but could only stare at him, unsure what to do. The leader was right: Murdock was not breathing. Simkins, still suffering from his first beating, crawled over to Murdock's limp body and administered mouth-to-mouth resuscitation. First-aid training had been mandatory for every driver when they arrived in Baghdad, including refresher courses every quarter. Simkins had never paid much attention, but it all came back to him now that it was needed. Murdock failed to respond. Simkins pounded his heart with a clenched fist before pressing his ear to his chest. Nothing. He pounded again, this time harder. Finally, a pulse...but faint. It was enough. Simkins resumed breathing into his mouth. The other men could only watch and hope. Some prayed.

After agonizing moments, Murdock took a breath on his own. Shallow at first before he coughed, then choked in huge amounts of air. The other men breathed a sigh of relief, elated that Murdock had been saved by Simkins' quick actions. This success was the only positive thing that had happened to them since their imprisonment. They wanted to celebrate but didn't dare, for fear of the repercussions.

The "reward" for this success was swift. The two men who had thrown Murdock in the cage moments earlier re-entered and pulled out the nearest prisoner. It would be his turn to suffer on the beating post. Their exuberance ended quickly—just the way the captors intended.

ℜ

After the truck had been concealed behind a cluster of bushes, Johnson headed toward camp. They would have to come back for the boar later. He was proud of what he had just accomplished. He'd survived an attack by a dangerous animal. He'd fixed the truck, risking his own life to do it. Then he put out a fire utilizing the only resource at his disposal—his own body. The companies that wouldn't hire him earlier that year were nuts. He still had plenty to offer. Nothing was going to stop him now.

As he moved slowly down the road, the limp more pronounced than ever, his wounded leg gave out and he fell to the ground, groaning as he hit the dirt. He pulled up his pants leg to take a look and didn't like what he saw. Much worse than the day before. The pain had increased, but he hadn't complained; nothing he could do about it anyway. Now, however, he realized it must be infected. Maybe there was some old-fashioned remedy Jabaar knew about that would help. He had to get back to the others, realizing his next steps would be some of the most painful he would ever have to take.

He continued along the road, listening intently in case someone else happened to be nearby—as unlikely as that was. He stayed close to one side so he could dive into the bushes to avoid being seen, if necessary. Each step was agonizing, but he had to get back. Too much depended on him.

When he rounded the last bend before he would have to start up the hill to the camp, Numley spotted him and hurried down.

"What happened, Charlie?"

"It's my leg. Hurts more than hell itself and looks even worse."

Numley helped him into camp. The others gathered around, concerned. They helped him lie down. Jacobs carefully rolled up his pant leg, then recoiled, gagging from the wound's stench.

Owens leaned in. "Not good. It looks like the pictures I saw of gangrene when I went through military training years ago."

Jabaar nodded. "This pretty bad all right. Surprised it got this way so quickly."

Jacobs asked, "Why didn't you say something, Charlie?"

"What would you be able to do if I had?" He rose up on one elbow. "Jabaar, I'm hoping you got some kind of remedy you can mix up for this thing. You know, from some roots or plants or something."

"Sorry. If home, I have something. Not here. Only thing I can do is put on mud. It might draw out poison. Coolness might give you comfort from pain."

"I'm game for anything at this point. Thanks."

Jabaar scooped dirt from a root hole and mixed it with water. He gently applied the mud to the wound. Even his light touch caused Johnson to flinch in pain. They didn't know if the mud would help, but if nothing else, it eliminated the stench.

Owens' concern about their undertaking had grown even more significantly since earlier that morning. He had learned years ago that gangrene—the name given to the death of tissue in a part of the body, usually an extremity—was fatal unless acted upon swiftly. Johnson had injured the lower part of his leg near the ankle, so his foot had the gangrene, though it was the actual wound where he felt the most pain. His gangrene was moist, as compared to dry, so in addition to the black dead tissue and the inflamed red healthy tissue next to it known as the zone of demarcation, his injury was covered with blisters that were oozing fluid—the reason for the disagreeable odor. The ultimate solution is amputation of the dead limb in order to save the rest of the otherwise healthy body. Owens knew this and shuddered at the thought. Could he—or any of the others—cut off Johnson's foot without medication?

This turn of events demanded a dramatic change in plans. "I was hoping for more time to make sure we were fully prepared before attempting the rescue. Charlie can't wait. We've got to move up our timetable and then get him to a hospital fast or this wound will kill him."

Owens didn't have the heart to tell Johnson that when they did get him to a hospital, they would probably have to amputate a major portion of his good leg. He would deal with that later. The other negative was that they would now be one man short. No way could Johnson help them. He thought that maybe by using a crutch, Johnson, rather than Jabaar, could return to the truck and drive it up to the entrance of the cave while the rest of the team attacked. That would at least give him something positive to do and keep him out of the way.

"We don't have a choice now. We've got to attack right away — tomorrow at the latest. Their supply truck should be coming again around noon." He looked at his watch. "We've got a little over an hour to get in place and commandeer it so Jabaar can scout out the cave and see what we're up against. Charlie, we'll take care of this. You stay here and make a crutch. You'll need it to get Rodney's truck when we attack."

"The hell you say! I can make a crutch in minutes. I'm going with you."

Owens shrugged. "OK, but your participation will be a last ditch effort. I lost your brother in Nam. I'm not going to lose you too."

"I wondered if you were the soldier that had dragged him back. Thanks for trying. And don't worry about me. I can take care of myself. By the way, I found these gloves in the truck, under the front seat. One of you can use them when you're climbing down the hole." He tossed them to Jacobs.

"Great…these will help a lot."

"Oh yeah, and I killed a boar. The bacon is in the back of the truck. A couple of you will need to drag it up here so we can have it for dinner tonight."

"*You* killed a boar?" Numley was dumbfounded.

"Yeah. I'll tell you about it later, I've got work to do."

Johnson borrowed Jabaar's knife to cut off a branch from a nearby tree for his crutch, in better spirits despite the severe pain — proud of what he had accomplished on his own. In fact, everyone's morale had improved since his return. They knew their plan had started to come together. And assuming success, they had a ride home.

ℜ

"We've run into difficulties trying to collect that much money in such a short period of time. Our sources are asking questions we don't want to answer. I've got some of it, but still have a ways to go. Can you stall them?"

Tom Randall hadn't slept all night worrying about getting the rest of the money from Murdock's assets and then delivering it in time to save his men. He needed to say something on the Baghdad TV Network as soon as possible so that the captors would know his company was serious about saving their lives. After several conversations with Buck Buchanan, Marine Base Commander, about how best to handle the situation, he was still in a quandary. If he announced that he had *all* the money, his company would know about it and call him with its own set of questions, questions he didn't want to answer, as he had not obtained their permission to gather more than the two million they had committed. How could he stall? He had not yet heard from the terrorists' contact person. And what if he announced that he only had two million dollars; would that be enough for the guy to call? All of these concerns were troublesome.

He had approached Commander Buchanan about proactively contacting the terrorists through one of his own informants, but to no avail. They didn't know which cell to contact. This was the best-kept secret in Baghdad.

At the moment, Randall decided he could only announce that he had the two million dollars provided by his company. It had arrived several hours earlier. If he decided, to hell with what corporate thinks, and mentioned more, and it didn't arrive, it could make matters worse for the hostages. He needed to wait for confirmation.

Randall replied, "If you can round it up today, when will you be able to deliver it?"

Murdock's representative said, "Our goal is the Baghdad airport by mid-morning tomorrow. Our jet will fly all night. Will that be in time?"

"I don't know. I'll do the best I can. Call me when the money is in the air."

ℜ

The old guys moved quickly to be in place before the supply truck arrived. They knew their tasks and were in their assigned locations well before it was expected. This included the digging of a shallow grave for the driver; they could not risk sparing his life. A gruesome thought, but reality. With the severity of Johnson's wound, they wouldn't have time for a second attempt if this one failed because they'd tried to spare a life in the process.

The assault would take place approximately one mile from the cave. If the driver didn't stop, rather than slitting his throat as planned, Owens would shoot him as he drove by. They would have to risk that shot being heard, although at this distance, they doubted it would be heard in the cave.

Jacobs would then jump on board and stop it before it ran into anything. They needed that truck.

Assuming the driver did stop, they would attempt to learn the signal for that day. If he resisted, Owens would make it uncomfortable for him until he divulged it. In the end, one way or another, his throat would be slit with Jabaar's knife.

Jacobs and Johnson were stationed in the bushes on one side of the road, Numley and Owens on the other. They spread out, not knowing until the last second where the driver might actually stop. They figured it would happen within ten to fifteen yards from where Jabaar would enact his part of the plan.

A half hour later they heard the sound of the approaching truck. Their adrenalin soared. This would be their first life and death action with the enemy. Other than Owens, none of them had killed a human being before, much less contemplated it. Now, one of them would be doing just that. It was a chilling thought; each hoped it wouldn't be him. Still, so much hinged on this first phase of the plan.

Jabaar staggered down the middle of the road half naked, as if he were injured, crying out for help. He had to be convincing, or the driver would just run over him or shoot him. They needed the driver to stop, get out of his truck and investigate.

The truck, traveling faster than before, made it even more dangerous for Jabaar. Owens raised the rifle and took careful aim at the driver's head, ready to pull the trigger. The truck screeched to a halt just short of hitting Jabaar. The driver emerged as Jabaar, with a final cry, fell to the ground.

The driver cautiously approached the still body while looking around. This could have been a diversionary tactic often used by bandits. With pistol drawn, he bent over to look at Jabaar.

Johnson, the closest to them, leaped from behind the bushes, his crutch flailing wildly. He exclaimed, "You son-of-a- bitch—"

The driver turned and fired at Johnson as his crutch found its mark. Jacobs, a step behind, kicked the gun from the driver's hand then pinned him. Johnson fell in a heap next to them.

The driver, now securely held by both Jacobs and Numley, screamed obscenities. Owens approached, shouting, "Shut up, scum bag!"

The driver glared at him. Owens kicked him in the stomach.

"Now, tell us asshole, what's the damn signal today?"

Jabaar, who had gotten to his feet, said, "He does not understand you."

He knelt by the driver and asked the question in Arabic. The man shook his head; he wasn't about to tell them anything.

Owens grabbed Jabaar's knife and plunged it into the driver's hand. He screamed in agony, but it wasn't enough to make him talk. Owens moved the knife back and forth;

more screams, but still no information. Wrapping his arm tightly around the driver's neck, he placed the tip of the knife under his right eye. "Tell him this is his last chance. If he doesn't tell us, he'll be blind before he gets to Paradise."

Jabaar translated. In great pain, the driver refused again.

Owens released him and said softly, "Sorry pal. Third time's not *your* charm." He grabbed him by the hair, pulled his head to the side and stuck the knife deep into his neck, twisting it as it struck the spinal cord where it connects to the brain. Less blood than a slit throat.

He slammed the body on the ground face up to ensure the small amount of blood oozing from his neck would not stain his camouflaged shirt. Jabaar would wear that shirt, as well as the pants, when he entered the cave. They were quickly removed.

Jacobs cradled Johnson's head in his arms. He had been hit square in the chest.

Johnson wheezed, "I think I screwed up, boys."

Jacobs replied, "You did good, Charlie."

Owens squatted next to them, saddened. "Damn it Charlie, this didn't need to happen. If you had just followed my orders…damn it all to hell!"

The others gathered around him, stunned. Johnson whispered a few more words about a white light, and about seeing Ruthie. "Win, guys. Don't let those bastards…get away with this. You…gotta win!"

He let out a last gasp, and was gone.

No one moved. Tears flowed freely, heads bent low in shocked silence. All they could do was stare in disbelief at his still body. They knew there would be risks in their decision to follow the captured drivers, but losing one of their own *before* the actual rescue attempt brought a renewed reality to this dangerous mission. All of them could be dead tomorrow.

Owens was the first to stand. "Guys, you heard Charlie. We've got a job to do. Let's go. They'll be suspicious if the truck is late."

"But what is the signal? If I say something wrong, they will kill me."

Owens shrugged. "I know. Let me think about it. Right now let's take a look at these supplies. Maybe there's something we can use."

Numley jumped into the back of the truck and started opening boxes and moving things around to get a better look. There were a couple of rusty old knives in a toolbox. They took one. Another weapon for the attack. There was also food. They took some to complement the boar they would have for dinner that night. Johnson would've enjoyed that.

They found a box of ammunition for an AK-47, but no rifle. "Shit." Owens shook his head. "The least they could have done was include a damn rifle. Well, we're no worse off."

Three cans of gasoline were found. "We'll keep one of these cans. In case Jabaar doesn't come out, we'll put it in the other truck and one of us can drive back to Iraq for help."

Owens used a stick to determine how much gas was left in the tank. He wasn't about to trust the gauge. He found it over half full.

"Great news. Assuming we can siphon gas out of their generator, we can drive both trucks back to Baghdad."

Jabaar took a closer look the dead driver and said, "Don't know if a problem or not, but this is the same driver from first time."

Owens said, "I thought he might be. His shirt gave him away."

Jacobs shrugged. "Not much we can do about it now. If this truck doesn't show up, they'll wonder why. Probably send someone out to investigate."

"We don't need that. We're going to have to take our chances. We've got to know what we're up against once we get inside. You're still game, right?"

Jabaar nodded. He knew how important the information would be, but still wondered about the signal.

Jacobs had picked up the dead driver's pistol. "Guess this is the only additional gun. Do we keep it or give it to Jabaar?"

"It won't be much help out here if this thing falls apart," Owens said. "And they might get suspicious about an unarmed driver they don't even know. Give it to him."

"Look." Numley lifted up a blue plastic sheet that had been bunched up in a corner behind one of the boxes. "Here's a tarp for Charlie."

Although they didn't like the idea, Johnson's body would have to stay in the bushes until they could take him home.

Owens said, "Why don't you and Keith wrap him up and hide him while Jabaar and I get rid of the driver's body?"

After they were done, Jabaar finished buttoning the driver's shirt and got in the truck. Owens said, "Here, wrap this cloth around your head and face. It might make you look more intimidating."

They climbed aboard the truck and rode with Jabaar, stopping a few hundred yards from the cave. As they got off, Jabaar said, "I am still worried. What signal should I use?"

Numley said, "Don't worry Jabaar, you'll be OK."

"That easy for you to say."

Owens touched Jabaar's shoulder. "After thinking about it, they'd probably keep it simple. Use the one this driver used the first day. Do you remember it?"

"Yes. I know."

He nodded and smiled at him. "Good luck in there."

Jabaar waited a few moments to give the others time to get in place. He had practiced how to stand, how to look, even how to sound. Though they were in Iran, where Farsi is the main language, this group spoke Arabic, the language of approximately eighty percent of the Iraqi people. There would be no problem with communication.

The truck drove up to the cave and, as before, the engine turned off. He had arrived on time. It was just past noon.

"Allahu Akbar," Jabaar shouted.

Silence. Nothing happened. The bushes remained in place.

Jabaar waited for what seemed like forever, then shouted again, "Allahu Akbar."

Again, silence for a few moments.

Then, the bushes parted. The truck drove in.

It had begun.

ℜ

If Jabaar was nervous, he didn't show it. He had been well coached by Johnson. He was going to miss that man. He parked the supply truck just inside the cave, and several of the terrorists began to unload it. The two cages with the drivers stood in front of him. They got up when he drove in, then slowly sat down. They'd probably hoped it was a rescue, but realized it was just the supply truck again.

One of the terrorists asked, "Where's Baruk? He was supposed to drive today."

"He's sick. They told me to drive."

This question had been anticipated and hopefully they had come up with the right answer. It was often common for terrorists in hiding to be sick. With a dwindling food supply, they were prone to illness. As many of them were from surrounding countries, they were outcasts within the towns and villages they had inhabited—although feared by the residents. They had to steal what they needed to survive by overpowering the locals. The occupation of Iraq by foreign terrorists was bad for everyone.

Jabaar's answer must have worked, because the man asking the question just nodded and walked off. As he answered the question, Jabaar noticed one of the others staring at him intently. With head cocked, he stroked his chin as if trying to remember something. The only one with a mask on, his stance looked vaguely familiar. This observation was terrifying. Did this terrorist know him? What if he was recognized? He didn't look that much different, even if his face was partly hidden by a headscarf and scraggly beard. He turned slightly to hide his face even more in the rag around his head. He knew that he would be trapped in the cave if this man figured out who he was. What could he do?

"You!" Jabaar suddenly shouted. "Be careful with that box you're carrying. If you drop it, the ammunition inside can explode and you'll kill us all."

The man's eyes opened wide and he didn't question the driver's command, carefully setting the box down with the other boxes and the two cans of gasoline that had already been unloaded.

The man in the mask, evidently satisfied that he need not be concerned with this new driver, turned toward the caged prisoners, glared at them, then slowly walked to the back of the cave.

Jabaar took a deep breath and looked around the cave to memorize as much as he could.

The two cages were positioned with one slightly to the left toward the front of the cave, the other almost all the way to the back. The prisoners in the rear cage were naked, the marks from their beatings clearly visible. He did not allow his face to disclose what he felt.

Jabaar surmised that the vent hole must come down behind the back cage, as the generator was next to it and he couldn't see the exhaust hose. Two boulders stood behind the rear cage, one along the side, and two others closer to the entrance. The terrorists appeared to congregate in the area between the two cells. The lights were positioned there, and that was where they cooked their food. They also had a television. He saw a video camera pointed toward a post with straps at the top. As he looked closer, he could see blood on the post, with large dark stains on the ground around it. His stomach knotted. He had seen his neighbors beaten many times on posts just like that. After taking a deep breath to regain his composure, he saw two large crates next to the boulder on the right.

Studying and memorizing his surroundings as nonchalantly as possible, he noticed a large coil of rope lying on a rock in front of the truck. He knew his American friends could use that rope, and he needed to remove it without raising suspicion. But how?

He thought, *Just take it.*

The men nearest him were still unloading the truck. Jabaar moved over to where the rope was coiled and picked it up. It was heavy, probably quite long. Maybe a couple of hundred feet...more than enough to reach the floor of the cave, he guessed. He put his arm through it and began to tie a knot at one end as he slowly started back toward the truck.

He had only taken a couple of steps when strong arms grabbed him from behind, holding him firmly. "Where is the other can of gasoline? And what are you doing with that rope?"

ℜ

"So your people still don't know any more than they did two days ago?"

Randall, frustrated with the lack of information from the military, continued his conversation with Commander Buchanan. "I just got the two million from my company. The rest might come in tomorrow morning, if they can get it. To make sure the terrorists know we are trying to comply with their demands, is there any chance the Iraqi prisoners can be released?"

Buchanan got up from behind his desk. "Our position about freeing prisoners is the same as always. Even if they captured the President of the United States, we will not negotiate with terrorists for the release of any hostages. As our Secretary of State reminds us, to do otherwise only encourages them. We feel bad about this and are empathetic toward your captured employees and their families. But if we start to negotiate at this stage, it will prompt a greater number of attacks on our people. They will take even more hostages, delaying Iraq's efforts to gain enough control with their own government for their ultimate democracy. That alone will prolong our stay here. Our country can't let that happen."

"I understand the reasoning. I just feel so helpless, and want to make sure I have personally done everything possible."

"You've already done more than your company as far as the money is concerned. All you can do now is what you already planned—a live television broadcast announcing that you have two million, and why it's not the full amount demanded. If it's acceptable to them, you should be contacted rather quickly. It's your call whether you want to hint about the additional money then, that it will take more time. This public request for money tells me this must be a small, under-funded splinter group of al-Qaeda. A couple of million dollars right away might be enough to get your men back in one piece. I don't have any other ideas. As you know, we haven't stopped looking. I've had planes fly out to the camp every day to explore the terrain. In fact, I even had them fly *past* the camp all the way to the Iranian border yesterday, just in case we missed something."

Randall said, "Thank you for your continued efforts, Commander. Skip and I were out there that first day, along with your investigators. They didn't have much of anything to report."

"I personally went out as well. As you know, after a thorough investigation, all the signs indicated that the terrorists brought the captives back toward Baghdad, or at least back in this direction to hide them. But they haven't been seen by anybody. Nothing that even looks suspicious. It's almost like they've evaporated into thin air. We checked satellite surveillance too, but it wasn't positioned to gather information out there that night."

Buchanan continued: "Although the explosion was large, they weren't very sophisticated as they used far more explosives than they needed to demolish the place. The unexploded dynamite we brought back to the lab was nondescript. It could have been obtained anywhere in the Middle East. The clock, for what that's worth, was a cheap private label type sold through many discount stores." He chuckled. "It seems that even the terrorists look for bargains. It's amazing the rest of their clocks worked as well as they did. I wish we had more, but we don't. I will call you the minute I hear of any developments. I would love to beat these bastards, just once, at their own game — turn the tables on them in a huge public way. That would be a big shot in the arm for our troops. A big morale booster for them, and in fact *all* Americans. We want those men back as much as you do, and in one piece."

Randall nodded. "I'm heading over to the TV station right now to announce that I have the two million. Wish I could say more. Sure hope it doesn't piss 'em off. Thank you again for your diligence, Commander."

ℜ

Jabaar struggled. Then, he relaxed his body as he looked at the supplies. "I don't know where the other can is. Somebody must have already taken it to the back."

"Everything from the truck is right here. We always get three full cans. We always send back three empty cans."

"Maybe it fell off. The road is narrow and rough. I had to stop and pick up some supplies that fell off when I hit a big hole. Maybe the can rolled into the bushes. I don't know. If someone wants to come with me, we can go back and look. I think I remember the spot."

"None of my men leave the cave."

"All I know is, it's bumpy. Next time, I think the supplies should be tied down. Unless you need the rope here?"

The man released him and turned him around as he spoke. "The rope is no longer needed. Make sure the next delivery is tied down tight. And tell them we need four cans of gasoline tomorrow."

"I will." And he threw the rope in the cab. The man continued to stand there and watch.

Jabaar had seen enough. No need to make them any more suspicious than they already were. He waited by the back of the truck for the last remaining boxes to be unloaded. One of the henchmen ran up to his assailant.

"Ali, come quick. They are making an announcement about the money."

Jabaar followed them, staying a short distance behind. He thought it would be important to know what was being said. He peered at the television and saw Mr. Randall stating that the military would not release the Iraqi prisoners and would not be leaving Iraq any time soon. He said that he did have two million dollars for the release of his men...that it was all he could afford to offer at this time because the trucking company had already lost so much money there.

Ali slammed his fist loudly against the bars of the back cage. "The American infidels will be sorry they did not respond better to our demands."

He spat on the ground as he pointed at Jabaar. "You! Tell Sahir that I will personally kill the next prisoner tomorrow."

As he turned back to his men he added, "The infidels...they never learn."

ℜ

"Where the hell is he? What's happening in there?" Jacobs said to no one in particular.

Numley shrugged. "He's been in there for almost an hour. The other two were out in half that time. Something's wrong, I just know —"

One of the captors emerged, gave the all-clear signal, and the bushes parted. The truck appeared with Jabaar at the wheel. He nodded and drove off down the road.

At a pre-designated location, the equivalent of several long blocks away, Jabaar pulled to the side of the road and waited for the others. When they arrived, Jabaar, standing tall and looking proud, could hardly wait to tell them what he had learned. "There are seven terrorists. Six we see at camp plus one more. I think maybe he is inside man."

"What makes you think that?" Owens asked.

"He is only one with mask on. I wonder why. Decided he does not want drivers to know who he is. He seemed familiar. Scary moment when he look at me as I got out of truck. I think he for sure recognize me. But I fool him. He probably helped from beginning. I think maybe he is a traitor."

"That's good to know. Now, tell us about the layout."

Jabaar described the cages and the boulders behind them. "Maybe you hide there before attack." He told them about the television and video camera.

Jacobs shook his head. "Well, if they are anything like other terrorist groups, they probably videotaped their demands and made sure everyone watching could see their prisoners."

"They did, but I will get to that in a minute. Men were in both cells. Could not tell why they were separated. Most in front cell. Only four in back. No clothes on. Could see they were badly beaten. On right side of cave, two large crates. Not see very well. In shadow."

Numley said, "Probably not important. But, I like the sound of those rocks to hide behind during the attack. The more protection the better."

Owens nodded. "I knew it. I knew they'd be beaten. Let me check out the driver's pistol. We'll need to use that."

Jabaar handed Owens the gun, which he inspected with the precision of the drill instructor he had once been. He pressed the release on the left side with his thumb and swung the cylinder out to check the number of cartridges remaining. He then looked down its barrel before swinging the cylinder back into firing position.

"I wonder where they got this. It's a good ole American-made Smith & Wesson; double action six cylinder .357 Magnum with a three-inch barrel. It's not the cleanest weapon I have ever seen, but that can be remedied. What I can't change though, is it only has five bullets. The driver used one to kill Charlie. Couldn't find any more ammunition in his pockets, so that's it."

Owens took a closer look at the handle. "Well I'll be. Look at the notch here. This is Butch Simkins' gun! Remember him bragging about it? The terrorists must have taken it from him and then gave it to the driver when he made that first delivery. Probably wanted him to be able to protect their supplies."

Then he looked at the words underneath the cylinder on the right side and laughed. "Damn, this is a *Lady* Smith. Can you believe it? Butch was carrying a girlie gun. It looks like he tried to file off the word Lady, but it's definitely a Lady Smith & Wesson. I don't think Butch would want that getting around, do you?"

Numley said, "I'd like the chance to make sure everyone finds out."

"Amen," Owens said. "Just don't get caught. Anyway, this is a great firearm. Powerful, but its range for accuracy is limited. If you have to fire it, rest your hand on something for stability. If you hit something, I guarantee you it will stay hit! You two will have this when you attack from the rear. It'll come in handy if you can't round up a rifle or two."

"Understood."

Jabaar said, "About their television, I watch Mr. Randall announce he only had two million dollars for release of men. They *very* mad. Plan to kill prisoner tomorrow."

"That means we've got to go in before that happens." Owens said flatly.

"Oh, that reminds me. I was able to bring something out of cave. Think you maybe like it."

He reached inside the truck and brought out the rope. "Will this help?"

"Unbelievable!" was all Jacobs and Numley could say.

The relief that showed on their faces when they saw the coil of rope said it all. With all their hard work, they had still only been able to make about ten feet out of roots. This solved their most immediate need.

Owens praised Jabaar for his work, "You did great in there. I'm proud of you. Another question though: could you tell whether the floor was level, or did it descend into the cave?"

"Looked level, like road in front."

"That's good. Our guess about the depth of the hole should be close. What about the layout? Can you draw a picture of it?

"No problem." Jabaar sketched the cave in the dirt.

The Cave

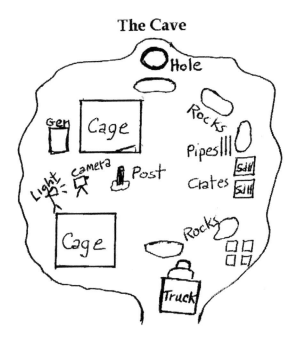

"We go in tonight. Zero hour is midnight. We'll start with the two of you lowering yourselves down that hole."

Numley said, "I've been thinking about this plan of ours. Now that we have the supply truck with gas, why don't we just drive it back to Baghdad and contact the military?"

Owens shook his head. "I thought about that, but our other problem is their friends, the ones that send the supplies. They're going to miss this truck real soon. We need to be out of here when they come to look for it. We don't need the odds to be any worse than they already are."

"But are we ready? I thought we'd have more time. I don't feel comfortable yet." Numley's concern showed.

"I know you aren't quite physically ready yet, but now that we have this rope, I think the drop can be made easier than we planned. I've got an idea."

Owens had Jacobs hold one end of the rope as he walked down the road with the other end. After it was stretched tight, he walked back, counting his paces.

"It looks like it's more than long enough to reach the bottom of the cave. Here's my idea. We cut off the extra portion and tie it around your chest. Before going after the two trucks, Jabaar will hold on to the rope and help ease you down the hole. The extra support will make you feel lighter. You'll only have to hold up half your body weight, so you won't need as much strength to keep from falling. The only thing you'll have to remember is to slide out of the rope before you drop to the floor so it can be pulled up for the next guy. This has to make you feel better, right?"

Jacobs and Numley looked at each other and shook their heads. Tonight was the night. There was no way out of it.

ℜ

The informant had pulled Ali over to a corner. "Damn those rich American infidels. They try to buy their way out of this with two million dollars. It's an insult."

"Both of us know they have lots more money for something like this," Ali said.

"They must pay dearly for this error in judgment."

"Yes, and they will. As I have already decided, tomorrow one of their people will be tortured, and I will personally take off his head."

"And by Saturday it will be on television so they can see what it cost them."

Ali added, "After the world watches, they'll change their minds about the thirteen million before anyone else is killed. The public will demand it. Even though some of the infidels will already be dead, we will get our money, and it will be the full amount—and the deadline begins at midnight!"

ℜ

The group responsible for sending daily supplies to their brethren in the cave would indeed be suspicious if their truck did not return as scheduled. Sahir Umar, the strategic mastermind and a stickler for details, ran the support group for the al-Qa'ida attack force, operating out of a small village southwest of Khorramabad—deeper still in Iran. It took about five hours under good conditions to travel over the rough road to the cave. By leaving at seven in the morning, the supplies could be delivered around noon each day. The truck would then immediately return to the village. Upon returning from the first run, the videotape of the demands had been delivered and subsequently sent to the three television stations for broadcast.

Sahir had carefully designed every phase of the plan. He expected precise execution; he was the reason this small group of Muslim extremists had accomplished what they had during its three years of existence on limited funds. Ali, already a trusted al-Qa'ida leader, had earned his respect. Sahir considered Ali his preeminent student. The current assignment—capture and hold for ransom a dozen

Americans—was the largest and most important mission ever contemplated by this group. Its ultimate success would propel Ali to the top of the al-Qa'ida organization.

The plan had been executed to perfection and Sahir was pleased with what had taken place. The next steps, already in progress after his recent call to the assigned intermediary, would fill their coffers with enough wealth to continue on for years. Nothing could be allowed to interfere.

"It is after eight. I ask again, has anyone seen Baruk?"

Sahir had been meeting with senior officials all afternoon and into the evening hours. He had asked about Baruk during each break after six o'clock. The man had not returned, a fact that he now found highly distressing. It wasn't according to plan. The truck selected was their best vehicle and had been well maintained. Mechanical difficulties were unlikely. If Baruk had been accosted along the way, all he had to say was that he traveled under specific orders of Sahir Umar, and he would be allowed to pass. That was how powerful Sahir had become in the region. So what had delayed his arrival? He didn't dare wait any longer to find out.

"Gather the men, we're taking a trip. Both trucks. And mount the machine gun on mine. We leave at nine."

They would get to the cave around two in the morning. Under his breath he added, "This plan must not fail."

ℜ

The phone rang for the ninth time in the last hour. Randall started to have Schick tell the caller he wasn't there, but changed his mind. This was a difficult time, and he had to be available for everyone until he got his men back.

He picked up the phone and quickly sat down. It was the intermediary assigned to make the arrangements for the delivery of the money. The conditions were that no one but Randall was to know about the conversation.

"I've got two million now. But what I didn't say on TV was that I may have the rest tomorrow morning, which meets your deadline."

"*Their* deadline. I am just a humble servant...a trusted friend. When will the rest of the money arrive?"

"They thought it should be here about mid-morning."

"I will call you then."

"Wait a minute, once I have the money, then what?"

The contact person had already hung up.

ℜ

After they'd eaten the boar meat along with the food commandeered from the supply truck, Owens said, "We should try to get some sleep before we go in. Tomorrow's going to be a long day."

He described what they would likely experience, and that they were about to risk everything. Their futures—if they had a future—would be decided during the next several hours. "I know you're scared. So am I—but so will they be, at the first shot."

Surprise was their advantage. It would take the terrorists a while to respond, all the time the three of them needed to get the upper hand. He assured them that with their adrenaline working overtime, they would have more than enough strength to accomplish the mission, with or without the additional help from Jabaar and the support rope. The gloves Johnson brought from the truck would help them scale down the rope. The first one down needed to tie them to the end of the rope to be used by the other climber.

"The climb down will be the least of our worries. It's what we do inside the cave that will count the most. Everyone has to stay cool. We need to be thinking at all times. In fact, we need to try and think *ahead* of the action."

Numley said, "That's not so easy for us. You've done this type of thing before. We haven't!"

"I know. But even though I've been in firefights before, it's just as dangerous every time. And remember, you've been trained by a Marine—a crash course for this specific operation. No one wants to die, so we have to operate as a team. It's the only chance we've got.

"In my opinion, the measure of a man is not that he has fallen, but how well he picks himself up. I put a lot of pressure on you this week—for your own good. Each one of you has fallen, but you've gotten back up impressively. You're ready, and I'm willing to bet my life on it."

Owens' next words surprised everyone. "In a few hours we will attempt something very challenging. In case I don't make it and you do, I want you to find a special lady that used to be in my life and tell her my last thoughts were of her. Her name is Kathleen, but I called her Kate. We met in school before I went into the service. She was slender with beautiful black hair and a style that melted my heart. We were inseparable. I almost told her that I loved her, but didn't because I had enlisted in the military and was leaving the end of summer. I was young and immature, and although we'd been dating for several months, when I stopped by her home as a surprise one afternoon, another boy was there. I was so jealous that I quit asking her out. Later I learned that she didn't know why we had stopped dating. She was confused and hurt as much as me. But neither of us had the sense to talk about it.

"I had a second chance years later, but screwed that up too. I had just gotten a divorce and wasn't thinking straight. I was a real ass in those days, especially when it came to women. I haven't seen or talked with her since, although I think about her on a regular basis and remember all our good times together. I wish that I could tell her how sorry I am that I hurt her. I hope she's doing well, and even pray for her health and happiness."

The guys looked at each other, astonished. *Dave prays? Live and learn.*

"I've finally come to the realization that I wasn't worthy of her, otherwise we'd be together. If I don't make it, please look her up. She still lives in Southern California. Deal?"

"You got it, Dave."

"And one more thing. I wrote out my will before coming over here. It mentions a…friend and her child that I've made a personal commitment to help out financially. It's the main reason I'm over here. Make sure they receive their money.

The will is back at my place in Bishop along with the particulars about Kate."

"You're going to make it Dave, we all are!" Jacobs said. "We've come too far not to."

"Thanks, but I know there are doubts about whether or not our plan will work. I read somewhere that courage is holding on a minute longer. That's what we've got to do, hang in there a minute longer than we think we can. If it's any consolation, some of our greatest generals also had doubts about whether their missions would succeed."

The camp was silent for a moment as they pondered this. Jacobs finally said, "If no one minds, I'd like to pray out loud for our success."

Owens nodded . "Go for it!"

"Dear Father, we come before you with our lives in your hands, as they have always been. Your Will be done. Please forgive us for our sins, and be with us as we attempt to do something none of us thought possible just a few days ago. Give us the strength, power and intellect to overcome these enemies to free innocent people. Please forgive us in advance that we will need to end the lives of other human beings to accomplish this goal. We are peace-seeking Christians. They are Muslim radicals with a hateful agenda for torturing and killing others. We seek your guidance for success through your son, Jesus Christ. Thank you for listening. Amen."

The others responded with, "Amen." Even Numley.

ℜ

Nearly midnight; the phone had rung for over half a minute before Randall finally picked it up. "Randall here. What's so important at this hour?"

"The money is in the air. You said you wanted to know."

"Oh, sorry. That's great."

"Now what?"

"Their contact person will call me in the morning. I'll know more then."

"Let us know what else we can do. After the delivery, we'll wait in Frankfort for further instructions."

"Let's all hope we're not too late."

Day Seven – Friday, January 13th

A LMOST MIDNIGHT. It's time."

Hearing Jacobs' whispered comment to Numley, Owens nodded. "That's right. I'll wait at the entrance fifteen minutes for you to get down before I go in."

Although Owens wasn't good with words, he was proud of what this team had accomplished in a short period of time.

"We've worked hard to prepare for this moment. There aren't many of us, but our odds are greater than many tough battles that have been won by the underdog. General Eisenhower once said, 'What counts is not necessarily the size of the dog in the fight; it's the size of the fight in the dog.' Remember what you've learned and all of us will come out of this thing in one piece."

He knew they would need certain things to fall into place during the attack, and a lot of luck, for *all* of them to come through alive. There was no doubt in his mind that they would prevail. He just didn't know at what cost. With this in mind, he took Jabaar aside and said, "After you've helped them down the hole and moved the trucks into position, stay in the supply truck and wait for us to tell you it's all clear. If we don't come out within a reasonable time…get the hell out of here. Head for Baghdad and tell them everything that happened."

They blackened their faces with mud and ash from the cooking fire, then broke camp for the final time and headed to their assigned positions. Aided by a sliver of moonlight to guide the way, they climbed the hill to the hole that led to the back of the cave...and their unknown fate. Owens remained on the road, assault rifle in hand.

ℜ

As they prepared to drop down into the hole, Jacobs held up two twigs. "Rodney, if you remember, Dave told us to draw straws to see who goes first. Short one leads the way."

Numley reached out to make his selection, then stopped. "You know, I just thought of something. It's Friday the thirteenth. That's a very unlucky day. Maybe we should wait one more day to do this."

"Sorry pal, I've always liked this date. My dad was born on Friday the thirteenth." His dad used to say if he didn't have bad luck, he wouldn't have any luck at all. Jacobs decided not to mention that.

Numley reluctantly selected a twig—the short one. Jacobs didn't know if it was good or bad that Numley would reach the interior of the cave before him. The main rope had already been secured to branches laid across the opening so it would hang down the middle of the hole.

The descent depended on the accuracy of an estimate—the distance to the floor. The main rope had to be long enough to reach it, or at least come close. If they had to drop the rest of the way, they ran the risk of breaking something in the dark, as well as alerting the enemy. The goal was to stay in the center of the hole to avoid scraping off rocks and gravel along the way. With the help of the second rope — the support rope held by Jabaar — their confidence was high.

To say they were frightened would be an understatement; no denying that. But as Owens had promised, their adrenalin raged. That would definitely help. If this first part of the plan didn't work, they knew their fate. They would be discovered too soon, something too disastrous to consider. Both knew it would be better to just be shot and killed rather than taken alive and subjected to the terrorists' brand of torture.

Jabaar tied the support rope around Numley's chest and lowered the main climbing rope down the shaft. Numley, shaking visibly, put on the gloves, took a deep breath, and grabbed hold of the main rope. Jabaar began easing him down into the terrifying darkness.

ℜ

The farther down he went, the more intense Numley's thoughts became. What was he afraid of? Death? They didn't have that many more years to live anyway. Who was he kidding? Nobody wants to die, no matter how old they are. He envisioned a news headline describing their failure: *Old Guys Die in Cave!* For him, at least, it would be an exciting finish to an otherwise dull and mediocre life.

He thought about the previous day leading up to this moment. They'd hijacked a truck, killed the driver, and stolen some supplies. Oh yeah, and one of them died. He chuckled to himself…a normal day's work? Go figure.

Owens had the rifle, Jacobs the pistol, and he had a knife. One lousy knife. He had hoped for a rifle, if only they'd found one on the supply truck. But he had to admit that the hole was far too narrow to have something that large strapped on his back. He hoped to be lucky enough to find one of *their* rifles in the dark before the shooting started. He desperately wanted the chance to fire one of the AK-47s Owens had told them about. He remembered the warning about using caution to avoid hitting Owens when he came in from the front. Yeah, right! He had already decided he would blast everyone in sight before they got a chance to get him. Owens best keep his head down.

As Numley continued his descent, he began to scream inside with fear. His body was already drenched in sweat. His hands swam inside the gloves, forcing him to hold on even tighter for fear of slipping out of them and falling off the rope. The hole seemed to grow more narrow and darker, the deeper he went. That was when he thought about claustrophobia. Even though he had never experienced it before, maybe this extreme situation was bringing it to the surface. And if that weren't enough, although he wasn't normally afraid of the dark, he rationalized that under these circumstances *anyone* would freak out, as he was about to do.

His descent quickened as he attempted to reach bottom before passing out. As the hole continued to swallow him up, he struggled with his breathing. He took short breaths through his nose in an attempt to remain calm. He didn't know if the light-headedness was just from the darkness that surrounded him or something physical. He questioned himself and his capabilities. Maybe he couldn't do this after all. He thought about climbing back up the rope. The guys would understand. They knew he wasn't the hero type. What did they expect?

All of a sudden his legs began to flail. The sides of the hole had disappeared. He had emerged into the cave.

He hoped he hadn't been heard, that nobody looked back there with a flashlight until he could drop to the floor and hide behind the rocks Jabaar mentioned. But how high was he? He couldn't see anything. He had no idea how far it was to the floor. He couldn't take much more of this.

As he reached the end of the rope he stretched his toes down, trying to feel the ground. Nothing. Suspended in mid air, he knew he had to drop the rest of the way—and hope for the best. He swallowed and let go. Only two feet...like stepping off a high curb. He had made it down without being seen, or getting hurt. Luck was with him so far.

A moment later the support rope, the one that held him during the descent, came crashing down. It glanced off his shoulder and landed in a pile next to him.

Numley was furious. *How the hell could Jabaar drop the rope?*

ℜ

Jacobs and Jabaar looked at each other in disbelief. Numley had forgotten to slide out of the rope before dropping the rest of the way to the floor. They had no idea he was going to drop when he did. The action had yanked the rope from their hands.

Jacobs clenched his fists and scowled. "Can you believe this? Does the guy ever think? The asshole! Hope they didn't hear it down there."

Jabaar stood. "And no way to get it back. What you do?"

"I don't have a choice. I have to climb down there without support *or* gloves."

"Here, take shirt." Jabaar ripped his shirt open. "We tear in half. Wrap it around hands. Protection from rope burns. Better than nothing. I put on driver's shirt later. He not mind."

Jacobs thanked him as he wrapped the pieces of shirt around his hands. He sat down with his legs in the hole, grabbed the rope firmly and started to lower himself down. Within seconds he was out of sight.

ℜ

Numley moved as if in a trance. He gathered up the support rope and crouched behind the nearest rock. As he removed it from around his chest he suddenly realized that it had been his mistake. He knew he was nervous, and that clear thinking was difficult if not impossible. He rationalized that Jabaar should have held on tighter.

Now what was he supposed to do? How would Jacobs get down? Alone. He was now all alone. If he could only see better, maybe he could figure something out.

The noise of the generator startled him, but not as much as the glare of the lights. The illumination filled the cave as brilliantly as if the sun had just risen.

ℜ

Owens checked his rifle, making sure the safety was off for the fifth time, when the light streamed out of the cave entrance. Still on the road in front of the bushes, he could see all the way in.

He couldn't believe it. The lights had just been turned on at night—a first since their arrival. He now understood why they had kept them off after dark. Even with the protection of the thick brush they were clearly visible from the outside.

From a tactical standpoint the light would help him, but not necessarily his men inside. Owens would be harder to see, as he would be entering from the dark. The other two, however, would be in the light.

No matter, he would still go in. He looked at his watch. Five minutes past midnight. The actual assault was set for fifteen after the hour. But, of course, that was when they thought the terrorists would be sleeping. Clearly, they were not doing that now. His plan allowed time for Numley and Jacobs to climb down the hole and get in position. They had never considered the possibility that they would have to attack in the light. Retrieving one of their rifles seemed all but impossible under the circumstances.

Owens decided to move into position right away, ready to attack sooner—just in case. He needed to see and hear everything happening inside. He dropped to his knees and elbows and silently crept through the bushes, his rifle in front of him, ready to fire at the slightest provocation. His first objective: the protection of the large rock directly in front of him. Again he wondered why the hell they had turned on those damn lights.

ℜ

The bright lights startled the prisoners, temporarily blinding them. They leaped to their feet; ready for anything, instantly realizing that the norm had been broken. They didn't know what to expect.

Murdock whispered, "Everybody try and relax. This may not mean anything. Stay cool."

Simkins expressed his concern. "But what if it's Friday already? Their deadline. Somebody is going to die, and it will probably be one of us back here. We've pissed them off the most."

Murdock shrugged. "We don't know that for sure."

"We know it's not morning yet. They've never turned on the lights at night before."

"So it's different. There's still nothing we can do about it."

"If they try to pull one of us out, everyone should jump 'em," Simkins said.

"Then what? They'd just shoot us all. Whatever happens, we need to try and get through it as best we can. Worrying about it won't help."

They watched the terrorists closely for some clue as to what their fate might be.

ℜ

Numley carefully peered over the top of the rock. He hadn't been seen. They weren't looking in his direction when the lights came on, and now, with the prisoners standing, he would be even more difficult to see. It also helped that the area behind the rear cage was far enough away from the light that it stood in the shadows.

As he contemplated his next move he heard a noise behind him. Turning quickly, he saw Jacobs drop off the rope. Although still upset about the accident, Numley was relieved that Jacobs had been able to get down.

Jacobs told Numley, "Both of us were holding onto that damn rope. We didn't think you would jump off without first removing the support rope. Jabaar was holding on so tight, you almost pulled him down. I grabbed him just in time. He had no choice but to let go."

Numley shook his head. "Sorry."

"Forget it. We need to figure out what to do next. Look around. Time's running out. Owens is gonna be coming in."

They watched as two terrorists opened the rear cell and pulled out a driver, relocking the cage. It was Butch Simkins. They dragged him to the middle of the cave. Dried blood covered half his naked body. He had been beaten so badly that his face was almost unrecognizable, one eye swollen shut. He couldn't walk, although he tried, with a left ankle that was either broken or severely sprained.

As they dragged him over to the beating post he moaned "Not again...please, not again." He passed out as they tightened the straps. His limp body hung there—one bloody mass.

To ensure he witnessed the final phase of his torture, they doused him with water. His body shuddered as he came to.

Ali began to chastise Butch in broken English, softly at first, then louder as he became more forceful with his ranting. "So, you think you are a hero for saving your friend?" He pointed at Murdock. "You think maybe you are even a God for bringing him back to life?" He waited for a response. "No matter. That is a mistake I will correct."

Simkins started to talk, but before he could utter a word, Ali said, "Silence, infidel. I will tell you when you can talk. There is only one God, and that God is Allah. Allah never dies!"

He looked around at the others. "I will prove this man is not a God, he is not Allah."

"I know I am not a God!" Simkins cried.

Ali ignored the outburst. "You are indeed fortunate. This will be your last beating. When I am done with you, I will take you out of your misery. I will cut off your head."

He shouted at the caged prisoners, "Did you hear that, infidels? We are going to cut off his head and prove he's no God! And tomorrow, if our demands are not met, one of you will be next!"

He bent over to get as close to Simkins' face as possible. "The camera is running. We record this historic moment for all to see the strength of al-Qa'ida. I want the world to see what cowards you are."

Simkins appeared mesmerized by the threat of death. He blinked his eyes rapidly as Ali continued with his tirade: "The beheading can be swift or painfully slow—your choice. It depends *solely* on your cooperation. Tell me what I want to hear. Denounce your country on TV and death will be made easier for you. But if you continue to deny you are a spy helping the infidel soldiers take over my country, your death will be slow and as painful as I can make it. I will see to it that your death is far worse than the beatings."

Simkins raised his head slowly and looked directly into the eyes of his tormentor. "You say the camera is running now?"

Ali smiled. "Yes, right now...speak up."

"OK. If I am going to die anyway, what I have to say to you is—*fuck you, fuck your dumb-ass cause!*" He spit in Ali's face. "*You're* the coward. Any one of us could beat the shit out of you if given the chance. And whether I live or die, you lose...my country wins. *You're all cowards!*"

The men in the cell, led by Murdock, shouted, "Cowards. *Cowards!*"

Ali had been humiliated in front of his men. He hit Simkins in the face with his fist. Simkins spat at him again in defiance. Ali hit him a second time, then a third.

The other terrorists, sensing a turning point in the attitude of the prisoners, started their own chant. "*Qad-em...qad-em...qad-em.*"

"They want your feet. I give that to them right now."

Hitting prisoners on the bottom of their feet with wooden batons or metal pipes was a favorite method of torture by those who served the sadistic demands of Saddam Hussein. The blows were far more painful there than on other parts of the body, as that was where many of the nerve endings were located. Simkins was about to be subjected to one of the highest levels of torture known to man—by terrorists well trained in the art.

"He will beg me for death," Ali said. His men laughed. "Bring me one of the pipes for the beating...no, bring them all. I want everyone to enjoy this infidel's last moments with us."

He ordered the straps removed from Simkins' hands and his feet bound in their place. They positioned him face up on his back. He would see each blow before it landed. "Put your hoods on. No need for neighbors to identify us after seeing this on television."

Murdock, holding on to the bars for support, looked back at the others; all knew that this was the beginning of the end. But he would be damned if these bastards thought the Americans would go quietly. He again shouted, "Cowards! Cowards! *Cowards!*" The rest joined him.

He called to Simkins, not giving a shit what the terrorists thought anymore. "Good luck Butch. My prayer is it will be over quickly. Try to focus on something else. Anything but this."

ℜ

The man assigned to retrieve the pipes headed to the back of the cave where Jacobs and Numley hid. He placed his rifle on a rock, freeing his hands to pick up several of the four-foot iron pipes that lay on the ground.

"This is our chance to get another gun," Numley whispered.

Jacobs nodded. "We need to get it while he takes those pipes to the others."

Without a second thought, Numley quickly moved toward the rifle, about thirty feet away. It would take only seconds to retrieve it, but he knew he would be a wide-open target for several of those seconds.

As Numley reached for the rifle, another terrorist spotted him, shouted a warning, raising his own rifle to pick him off. Jacobs, fearing this possibility, had already moved to a second rock for a better view. He fired a round from his pistol, hitting the terrorist in the head just as he shot at Numley. The bullet missed Numley, ricocheting off the rock next to him and grazed Jacobs' left arm. Blood trickled from the wound. The terrorist fell to the ground...his gun silenced.

The quick action gave Numley just enough time to grab the rifle and take cover. He aimed it at another terrorist and squeezed the trigger. Nothing happened. He squeezed it again; same result. He couldn't believe his bad luck. The only gun he could get his hands on was out of ammunition.

Then he remembered: *Check the safety. Release the son-of-a-bitch with your thumb and try again.*

Numley released the safety and squeezed the trigger again. A quick burst of gunfire sprayed the cave. For the first time in a week, Numley smiled.

ℜ

When the shooting began, one of Ali's men had been standing out of sight next to the wall by the front cage, adjusting a light fixture to improve the quality of the videotaping. After he watched one of his brethren fall and heard the hail of bullets from a blazing gun in the back rip through the cave, he decided he could better serve his group by going for help — immediately. Unseen, he darted into the darkness between the cage and the wall, heading toward the front of the cave. He then ran along the front wall past a large rock located between the cage and the entrance. Still unnoticed in the flurry of action, he raced out onto the road just as Jabaar, dressed in the camouflage shirt of the dead driver and armed only with one of the knives found earlier, drove up in the supply truck. He leaped into the center of the road, his rifle pointed directly at Jabaar, and shouted in Arabic, "Stop, or I will shoot you."

ℜ

Owens had just crawled into the cave, taking a position on the right side of the large rock just inside the entrance, when Jacobs fired the first shot. He focused on the gunfire and did not notice the fleeing terrorist, who had passed by the other side of the rock.

As the militants had gathered in the center of the camp, there were no rocks close enough for their own protection. They grabbed their rifles and fell to the ground, firing at the intruders. The drivers dove to the far side of their cages in a desperate attempt to avoid the bullets.

Numley had dropped a second terrorist, who briefly rolled around in agony before taking his last breath. As a third one dove behind the dead body to use it as a shield, Jacobs, his hand stabilized on the rock, took quick aim and fired off a second round simultaneously with Owens' first shot—at the same target. Direct hits. As the bullets exited, blood spewed out both sides of his body.

Some of Numley's shots whizzed over Owens head, missing him by inches. Just what he was afraid of: a novice with an assault rifle. "Come on...short bursts. Take short bursts!"

As he shouted the warning, Ali looked over his shoulder and saw the other intruder next to the rock. He turned to fire at him but wasn't fast enough. Owens saw the movement and his M-16 ripped through him. Ali, the leader, was dead before he hit the dirt.

The remaining terrorists were in the crossfire, with three, then four more of them already down. Owens and Numley kept firing until the last enemy gun fell silent.

ℜ

The informant watched from darkness, standing behind the crates. As much as he wanted to be the one to personally kill Simkins—he detested the man—he knew it would be best if he weren't videotaped for the world to see. After this was over he would return to his old job to further the next cause. His alibi would be that he had escaped during the attack, and struggled to survive in the desert as he walked back to Baghdad. When he saw Ali, his beloved cousin and leader fall, killed by someone coming through the front entrance, he forgot about that and crept out from behind the crates toward a rock that stood between him and the infidel. As he rounded the rock, Numley, who had moved to the center of the cave, saw him and shouted. The warning came too late. A shot rang out. Owens fell to the ground, clutching his leg.

Focused on shooting Owens, the informant hadn't heard the warning and didn't even see Numley, now charging at him. The force of Numley's body slammed him into the rock. The pistol flew from his hand. They hit the ground, Numley on top. Pinned down by Numley's body, he was helpless. Numley pounded his face, hitting him again and again until his bloody eyes closed into unconsciousness.

Ripping the blood-soaked hood off his head, Numley recognized the man he had just overpowered, a man all of them knew from the trucker camp. This bastard was Colonel Abdul, supervisor of the guards.

Recruited by Ali shortly after the death of their families, he had joined the Iraqi Guard to be on the inside of the new regime. Educated and fluent in English, valuable under the circumstances, he quickly moved up the ranks. When the opportunity arose to hire and supervise guards at the newly established trucker camp, he knew it would be a perfect cover for an assault on the American infidels. It only took three months to gather enough information for his cousin to lead the attack, backed by the support of the Iranian group. Jabaar had said he thought the seventh man in the cave was an insider, a traitor to the new regime he had infiltrated. He had been right.

"No wonder they found it so easy to get into our camp. You made sure it wasn't protected. Time to pay now, you son-of-a-bitch." Numley hit him again.

ℜ

Once again the cave was silent. The caged drivers could only stand in awe of what had just happened. They couldn't believe it. Their captors were dead. They were free.

Jacobs looked over at Simkins and watched his body slump with relief.

"Jacobs," he whispered, "is…that you?" He spoke in a weak, raspy voice.

"Yep." He said. "Do you still want that coffee, Butch?"

Simkins managed a laugh. "When we get back…" He took another breath. "…I'll be making *you* the coffee. You got here…just in time. They were going to cut off my head."

"Yeah, we know. We debated whether to attack before or after that happened."

"I don't blame you." Simkins took another deep breath. "Thanks for making it *before*."

"We weren't going to let them kill you if we could help it. And to think our country made a big deal out of clothes taken off some of *our* prisoners in Abu Ghraib. There's no comparison."

"And these guys didn't just point at our balls, they kicked 'em up into our throats." Simkins shook his head, "Man, am I glad you're here."

Jacobs removed the straps from Simkins' ankles and helped him to his feet, handing him one of the pipes to use as a cane. He then searched a dead terrorist and found the keys to the padlocks. As he headed toward the rear cell, another terrorist that they assumed was dead opened his eyes. The man still clutched his rifle tightly. He rose up slowly on one knee to take aim. But before he could fire, the slashing blow of an iron pipe landed against the back of his head and sent him to the ground. His neck snapped like the toothpicks Simkins chewed.

"Don't even think about it, asshole!" Simkins bellowed. "He's a buddy of mine."

Jacobs wheeled around to see Simkins standing over the dead man, the iron pipe held like a baseball bat. Simkins nodded at him; Jacobs nodded back in gratitude, then released the rest of the prisoners.

Murdock gave Jacobs a bear hug. "We'd just about given up hope. I should've gone with you to play cards. It would've been a lot safer."

Jacobs, thinking about the loss of Johnson, said, "That's debatable."

After performing a quick body count, Jacobs asked Murdock to confirm that they had killed all of the terrorists.

There were five dead bodies on the ground, plus Colonel Abdul. Murdock shook his head in disbelief. "Shit. Where's the seventh one?"

℞

Jabaar hit the brakes as he spotted the rifle-wielding terrorist. At first he had no idea what to do. He carried only the rusty old knife taken from the truck earlier.

"Don't shoot," Jabaar shouted.

The terrorist moved in closer to get a better look at Jabaar and apparently recognized him as the driver that had delivered supplies the day before. He likely remembered the camouflage shirt. Relieved, Jabaar again took on the persona of the driver.

"What are you doing out here? What is it you want?"

The terrorist climbed into the truck on the passenger side, saying that Jabaar needed to turn the truck around and drive as quickly as possible to their village for help, that they had been attacked. Men with guns had been able to get inside the cave and had killed the others. He felt fortunate to have escaped; Allah had blessed him. That blessing needed to be honored by severely dealing with the men that attacked them.

Jabaar, frantically trying to think of a diversionary tactic, replied, "I had an accident and was thrown from the truck. I think I broke my arm. That's why I returned to the cave. It is impossible to turn the steering wheel all the way around. Can you drive this truck?"

"Yes. Move over, quickly. I'm in a hurry."

The terrorist jumped out of the truck, ran around the front and climbed in on the driver's side. As he settled in behind the wheel, he put his rifle on the dashboard. Jabaar picked it up. "I'll hold the rifle in case one of them comes out to look for you before we're gone."

"Yes. Good idea—"

Jabaar smashed the rifle butt into the side of his face with such force that it killed him instantly.

He thought how stupid the terrorist had been to believe his story. "God blessed me, not him!"

As Jabaar pushed the terrorist from the truck, Jacobs ran out of the cave, rifle in hand. He watched the dead body fall hard on the dirt. "I was afraid he'd try to take the truck. Way to go, Jabaar."

After they dragged the body to the side of the road, Jacobs pulled aside the brush in front of the cave. "Bring in the big one…and back it in. It'll be easier to load."

ℜ

As the drivers put on clothes and drank water, Numley and Murdock attended to Owens, who still lay on his back after being shot by Colonel Abdul. The leg wound bled profusely, though it could have been far worse. Owens shook his head in an attempt to focus his eyes as he came to, having briefly passed out from the pain. The bullet appeared to have hit a blood vessel. Murdock worked on him until the bleeding subsided. Confident he had blocked off its major source, he had Numley make a tourniquet out of a dead terrorist's shirt. Pressure had to be maintained or Owens could bleed to death. A bandage to cover the wound was made with the rest of the shirt. The bullet had passed all the way through, so at least they didn't need to dig for it.

After Owens had been cared for, Numley looked at Jacobs' arm. "Don't worry. It's only a scratch. The bleeding has already stopped."

The noise of the truck's engine filled the cave as Jabaar backed it in. He climbed out and immediately saw Colonel Abdul lying on the ground; still unconscious from the beating he had taken from Numley. "Aag-eed. That is who looked at me strangely yesterday. I *thought* I knew him."

Owens, now up on an elbow, listened as Jacobs updated the others. "Jabaar got the last terrorist, but we still have a problem. We stole their supply truck. They've got to suspect a problem out here because it never returned. We need to leave as fast as possible to avoid being trapped in this cave when they come out to investigate."

He explained what needed to be done before they could depart.

The men who could walk went to work. They put all the gas that could be found into the tank of the truck. The strongest loaded the back of the truck with supplies — food, lots of water, the rifles and all the ammunition. Once the truck was ready to go, they took the dead bodies out into the bushes and hid them. They swept the dirt floor with brush to hide the blood from the dead terrorists but left the blood around the beating post, an ominous reminder of the prisoners' torment during the past week.

"If anyone does come to investigate, they might think the prisoners were taken someplace else," Jacobs said. "At the very least, it will give them something to think about while we get away."

As the others performed their tasks, Jacobs looked for communication equipment that could be used to contact the military. Because they were in Iran, even if he could contact someone, he feared they probably would not cross the border. His hope was they might be able to meet them *at* the border. He and his men would have to rely on their own ingenuity to get back to Iraq. It became a moot point. His search only turned up a set of walkie-talkies with minimal range.

They did find some sticks of dynamite along with blasting caps and a large coil of fuse wire. These had been carefully stored in the dark, and he almost missed them. Probably left over from their demolition of our camp, Jacobs thought. He picked up several sticks and showed them to Owens. "Should we take these with us?"

Owens, feeling stronger, grinned at Jacobs. "Bring it all. Never know…might come in handy. Keep it wrapped and carry it in the supply truck."

After checking the tourniquet again to make sure the bleeding had stopped, Murdock pulled Jacobs aside to discuss the two large crates still sitting next to the wall. To make it appear loaded, and hide the passengers at the same time, they would be placed at the back of the truck. If they were stopped along the way, the thought was that the crates might provide them with an excuse for being on the road, and at the very least, help them stall for time.

Murdock wanted to open them first. Both had the Iraqi Presidential Seal and Saddam Hussein's initials in addition to the words, *Do Not Open,* spelled out in Arabic and English. Hussein obviously wanted them left alone, and Murdock thought he knew what might be inside. "If I'm right, we'll be transporting a treasure back with us."

They pried the crates open. In the first one they found bars of gold worth millions. It also contained currency from various countries in addition to Iraqi Dinar, its worth difficult to calculate as it had dropped so much in value since the invasion. The other currencies were selected with care…euros, Spanish pesos and U.S. dollars.

Midway down was a briefcase wrapped in bubble pack. It contained six sealed vials, securely fastened in slots of protective padding made of flexible Styrofoam. If this briefcase had been accidentally dropped, the vials would not have broken. Murdock wondered how dangerous it would be to open one, but wasn't about to test fate.

From a historic perspective, the other crate contained the most valuable items. Murdock immediately recognized artifacts that had been looted from the National Museum in Baghdad during the days after the attack on that city. The Baghdad museum housed irreplaceable Babylonian, Sumerian and Assyrian collections that chronicled ancient life in the cradle of civilization, the area formerly known as Babylon before its name was changed to Iraq. Spanning a time from before 9000 BC well into the Islamic period, the Iraq Museum's collections included some of the earliest tools ever made by man.

Rumored as an inside job, the looting had obviously been pre-planned and highly organized. Items were removed from locked safes. The looters were equipped with glasscutters and keys to the museum vaults. Some hinted that Saddam Hussein had been responsible, as it was well known how much he cared for antiquities. It was said that if he were responsible for the initial looting, it would not have been to destroy the antiques, but to preserve them for himself. This discovery appeared to validate the rumor.

Murdock carefully extracted and unwrapped some of the contents, naming each as he did so. Many of the most beautiful items dated back to 3000 BC, handcrafted out of gold and copper. "These antiques are priceless. They need to be rewrapped so they won't be damaged."

Jacobs agreed, but it had to be done quickly. He assigned the task to Murdock.

They were almost ready for the final phase of their exit strategy. It had taken close to two hours to execute the attack, load the truck, fill its tank and hide the bodies. Charlie Johnson's wrapped body had already been placed in the back of the supply truck.

The rescued men, along with Owens, would be transported in the larger truck. Numley would drive that truck, with Jabaar and Jacobs following close behind in the smaller truck.

As the drivers prepared to climb aboard, Simkins saw Colonel Abdul move. "Looks like Colonel Asshole is waking up. What are we supposed to do with him? Can I shoot his ass?"

Owens directed them to take him along. "Don't worry, the Iraqis will know what to do with him. He'll stand trial as a spy and traitor to his country."

Before throwing him in the truck, they tied and gagged him. Someone would be assigned to watch him every moment. He wouldn't hesitate to kill any of them if given the chance; they had already seen that.

As the crates were about to be loaded, Jacobs leaned in and handed one of the walkie-talkies to Owens, who had been helped onto the truck. They would keep the volume low in case they were stopped along the way. Jacobs would follow as a moving lookout, keeping him informed about anything suspicious. Owens patted the rifle at his side. "If we run into any trouble, I'll be ready."

As Simkins climbed in, he looked over his shoulder at Jacobs. "Hey man, thank you for all this. I've been a real prick...and I'm sorry. Randall was right. You guys have a lot goin' for you."

"You can buy me a brewski when we get back, OK?"

"A six-pack, and I hope we can drink 'em together."

"Count on it. Let's get going. This has taken too long already."

Jacobs, Numley and Jabaar placed the two crates onto the lift at the back of the truck. As they thought, once in position the passengers were well hidden. The Iraqi Seal and Saddam's initials faced inward. No need to draw any more attention than necessary.

Numley started the truck. The engine's roar reverberated against the walls in the small confines of the cave. Both trucks would travel with their lights *out*.

Jacobs grabbed the video camera that had been turned off earlier and tucked it under his arm. He didn't know if he could use it, he just knew he didn't want to leave it behind as evidence of what had just happened.

After the truck cleared the entrance, the cave lights were turned off. Once outside, Jacobs and Jabaar pushed the bushes back in place. And as the terrorists had taught them, they brushed away the tire tracks of both trucks for about twenty yards in each direction from the entrance, making it difficult for anyone to know what had happened. Jacobs spent a brief moment fastening the camera to the dashboard before they set off after the others. He checked his watch: almost two a.m. Finally. They were on their way back to Baghdad.

As Jabaar put the truck in gear and sped off, Jacobs glanced back toward the cave. That's when he saw something in the distance: headlights.

ℜ

Although beat up and tired from the weeklong ordeal, the drivers were wide awake, but quiet, as the truck lumbered down the dirt road. Simkins broke the silence: "Hey Owens, if you don't mind, I have a question. Why did you risk your lives to help us...after the way some of us—especially me—treated you guys?"

Owens, now sitting comfortably with his leg elevated, said, "I think you've finally realized that many of you have acted like damn fools."

There was no answer, just bowed heads.

"I'll tell you why. It's who we are. It's how we were raised. Our parents were part of the greatest generation, according to newscaster Tom Brokaw. They taught us character. I'm ashamed to say many of the parents in *our* generation didn't do as good a job."

Owens had a lot of emotions and frustrations pent up inside since arriving at Camp Mojave. Simkins' question had opened the door for him to vent, and he was damn well sure he wasn't going to lose this opportunity to tell these young guys what he thought.

"Many of you looked down your nose at us because of our age. Maybe now you realize we're not twice as dumb as you, even though we *are* twice as old. With age, we also have twice the experience. We used it to save your asses."

He paused a moment, collecting his thoughts. "We were taught to respect our elders. We call them mister or missus until they tell us we can call them by their first name. All of this maintains tradition and helps to retain our American heritage.

"It didn't come naturally—parents demanded it. When it came to raising children, my ole man said, 'Either you run your kids or your kids run you...and no kid is going to run me!' Many parents these days think it more important to be *friends* with their children rather than disciplinarians. They also do their best to shelter them from real life. Children need the chance to solve their own problems, to overcome small failures so they can conquer the larger ones everyone faces later on. It builds resilience and makes them stronger. And the future of this country needs the new generation to be strong...as strong as our forefathers."

Owens took out his handkerchief and blew his nose. "America became the biggest, most powerful and best country in the world in a mere 200 years, surpassing large, well-established countries that had been in existence for over two *thousand* years. It didn't happen just because of our vast natural resources. Many countries have that. It happened because our forefathers established a government that centered on freedom for the people, while at the same time honoring God.

"Separation of church and state, declared in those early days, did not mean for us to eliminate God from our government, or from our schools or even from public lands. Its only intent was to ensure that religious leaders would never be able to rule our government like they did in Europe. 'In God We Trust' was intertwined into everything we did in those formative years."

He shrugged. "Some want God eliminated from our society. They fight to take '*under God*' out of our Pledge of Allegiance and stop children from praying in our public schools. Next, they will want to change our calendar, something recognized by almost every nation in the world—the one that is divided into two sections, BC and AD, Before Christ and After Death of Christ. These anti-Christian demands are only raised by a small minority in a country where 86 percent consider themselves to be religious. They ought to be told to 'stick it.'

"The worst, though, as we have seen first-hand, are those who demand that Americans convert from Christianity to Islam—or die. We're talking about radicals trying to take away our freedom, a freedom that applies to both men *and* women in America."

Owens seemed to be growing stronger with each new thought. "We can't let that happen! The flag of the United States of America stands for freedom—and always will. But it's up to every American citizen to make sure it stays that way! The older generation is almost gone. Keeping our freedom is now up to you, the younger generation and those who follow you.

"Democracies seldom have their freedoms taken away by an external force. They give them away 'one politically correct' piece at a time through legislative action and the courts, but also through appeasement. Appeasement cost millions of Jews and non-Jews their lives as England and France negotiated and hesitated before finally realizing that Hitler had to be fought, that his aggression could not be corrected by signing toothless agreements. Appeasement legitimized and stabilized communism in the Soviet Union, then East Germany, and then the rest of Eastern Europe where for decades inhumane, suppressive, murderous governments ruled."

He paused for a moment. "The war on terror will most likely last for generations. It's a conflict conducted by an enemy that cannot be tamed by tolerance and accommodation. In fact, these gestures encourage them as a sign of weakness. In ancient history, even Thucydides referred to this mistake: *'When one makes concession to one's enemies, one regrets it afterwards, and the fewer concessions one makes the safer one is likely to be.'* Think about this when you read a newspaper or watch the news that says America needs to negotiate with, and give in to, the enemy. Don't buy it for a moment."

Owens pointed at the stunned drivers. "Hopefully every time you see the American flag you will recommit yourself to preserving the freedom we all enjoy. Don't be silent and lie there letting others run over you, like the Muslim majority does when it comes to their radical brethren. All of us need to stand up for what we believe, to voice our concerns to our congressmen and other leaders. To silently stand by will permanently cost us not only our freedom of speech, but also all of the other freedoms we cherish today. We can't just depend on our military to defend our freedoms. You witnessed that a couple of hours ago when *we*, civilians, freed you. It's up to every one of us, every single day. Our future is counting on it."

As Owens finished, the others remained silent, thinking about what he had said, and how much it meant to each of them personally.

The crackling noise of his walkie-talkie broke that silence: "We're being followed."

ℜ

Sahir Umar and his trucks had come to a screeching halt in front of the cave, arriving just after the supply truck carrying Jacobs and Jabaar had sped off in the dark. With guns drawn, they'd crept through the bushes and cautiously entered the cave, not sure what they would find. Once it had been determined that the cave was empty, the lights were turned on to investigate it more thoroughly.

Everything of importance had been taken, including the crates for Saddam Hussein that were never to be touched, under threat of death. Sahir mused, "There were no signs of a struggle, so why would Ali move the men without first talking to me?"

He mentally went over a number of possibilities as one of his men rushed in. "Sahir, I have found a dead body hidden outside in the bushes."

"Search the entire area. Bring me information on everything you find."

He joined his men in the search, personally finding the blood-soaked body of Ali. As he grieved the loss of this exceptional student who had become his friend, he shouted to the sky, "This will not go unpunished. They will pay with their lives."

Now he knew the American hostages had escaped—that somehow they had been able to overpower Ali and his men. But how could this have happened? Every detail had been planned to perfection...nothing left to chance. How could fragile Americans, after almost a week of brutal beatings, have enough strength to overcome their captors? It didn't occur to any of them to check the exhaust hole, and the rope that still hung there.

One of his men told Sahir, "I found tire tracks...there." He pointed toward Iraq.

"As I thought. The infidels escaped in our truck. They try to return to Baghdad. That must not happen."

ℜ

"What do you mean we're being followed?" Owens shuddered. This wasn't over yet.

"As we left the cave, we saw headlights rounding the bend," Jacobs said. "A truck, I think. They didn't see us...we had our lights off. But they are right behind us."

"They would've stopped at the cave first. That will give us some time. Turn on your lights. We've got to kick into high gear."

"What do *you* mean give us some time?"

"What I mean is, give me time to think of something. We could be in some deep shit here."

ℜ

Sahir Umar, headlights blazing, traveled as fast as the winding dirt road would permit. He knew if the infidels reached Baghdad before he could stop them, all would be lost. As he pressed his driver for more speed, a loud explosion rocked his truck and it spun out of control. If not for the quick reaction of the driver, it would have rolled. Instead, it came to a stop just short of smashing into a tree on the side of the road.

A blowout — right front tire. Sahir jumped from the cab to examine it.

Totaled.

"How long to change it?"

He didn't like the answer.

Sahir grabbed his second in command. "You stay here and get this fixed. I will continue after them in your truck. Catch up as fast as you can. We may need the machine gun. Understood?"

"Yes Sahir."

Men were ordered to change the tire as Sahir and half the others pulled around the disabled truck to continue their pursuit.

ℜ

The sun peered over the hills on the two-truck caravan that had traveled most of the night carrying the old guys and the rescued drivers. They still had several hours to go before reaching Camp Mojave. Their ultimate objective of Baghdad would take two additional hours.

There had been no communication between the two trucks after Jacobs had notified Owens about the truck behind them. They traveled as rapidly as they could thinking that with enough lead-time they might be able to outrun them.

Jacobs had glanced over his shoulder often during the night, looking for the headlights, but thankfully saw nothing—until daybreak. "Owens. We didn't lose 'em. I can see their truck on the side of a hill. They're only a few miles behind us."

"Damn. OK, I have an idea. You've got the dynamite. How much fuse wire do we have?"

"It's in a coil. Looks like maybe eighty to a hundred feet."

"It'll be close, but should work. Be ready to stop on short notice. I'll tell the guys in here what we'll need them to do. We're gonna blow those bastards up. Let *them* find out what it feels like."

The trucks continued for another mile before suddenly stopping just beyond a bend in the road. Owens climbed out of his truck and directed Jabaar to back the supply truck into a small clearing and hide it in some brush. The lead truck parked farther down the road.

They popped the hood on the supply truck, and Owens quickly cleaned off the battery connections as Jacobs rolled out the fuse wire.

Owens said, "Hand me one end."

He fastened it to the negative side of the battery. "Run the other end out to the road. I'll be right behind you."

Owens limped as fast as he could onto the road. Finding a suitable location to plant the dynamite, he told Jacobs to take the other end of the wire back to the truck. It was just long enough. "Don't touch anything. I'll be right back."

He connected the blasting caps to several sticks of dynamite before connecting the wire. As he limped back, the others, assault rifles in hand, had already gathered around the supply truck. "Half of you go to the other side of the road. The others stay here. I want them in our crossfire."

He positioned them so they wouldn't hit one another when the shooting began. "Each of you pick a wheel and shoot it when the truck reaches this location." He pointed to the spot. "If the dynamite doesn't work, they'll at least be stopped. Then we shoot their asses as we see 'em."

He turned to Jacobs. "I want you to set off the dynamite. All you have to do is touch this end of the wire to the positive side of the battery. Do it when the front end of the truck is over the dynamite. I'm going to shoot at it as well. Between the two of us, it ought to go off. Any questions?"

ℜ

The wheels of the plane carrying the money touched down at the Baghdad airport earlier than expected, the result of tail winds. It didn't matter. Randall had been at the airport since sunup.

Money in hand, he sat by a telephone anxiously awaiting the call that would tell him where to take it. Although in an air-conditioned office, sweat covered his face and poured down his back. He didn't notice.

At last, the phone rang. He snatched it up. "Tom Randall."

"We are in business?" It was the same voice, that of the intermediary.

"I've got the money…all of it. Now what?"

The response came quickly. "Put it in a garbage bag and take it out to the installation you call Camp Mojave.

"It's no longer there. Your *friends* took care of that."

"Take it to that location. Place the bag under the remains of the eighteen-wheeler and then leave. You will need to be out there by noon."

"Will my men be nearby? Can I bring them back with me?"

"Your men will be released only after the money is safely in their captors' hands. After you leave the camp, the bag will be retrieved and the contents verified. You will then be contacted at your office. At that time, the location of your men will be revealed. It will take one additional day of trust on your part."

Randall scowled. "*Trust* these terrorists?"

"It is the only way. Will you deliver the money today or not? I must report back."

"I will be there…by noon. And pray to God I'm in time."

"And I will pray to Allah for the same thing. Move fast. It may already be too late for one of them."

"But how do I know they *will* be released?"

All Randall heard in response was a dial tone. The contact had hung up.

ℜ

The phone at Sahir Umar's headquarters in Iran rang until the intermediary finally gave up and placed the receiver back in its cradle. He had been excited to inform him of the additional money, that the full amount would be available at noon, complying with their demands. He thought it strange the telephone wasn't answered...by anyone.

ℜ

Owens and his men did not have to wait long. They heard the screeching of tires as the truck carrying the terrorists came barreling toward them. Jacobs turned on the video camera to record the encounter, hoping he would live to view it later.

As it rounded the bend, everything seemed to happen at once. Shots were fired from both sides of the road. Tires were hit, the blowouts sounding like small explosions. When the front bumper passed over the dynamite, Jacobs touched the wire to the battery. Owens fired an instant later. The dynamite exploded, sending the truck into midair, both doors of the cab flying open at the same time. It landed on its side.

"Now *that's* an explosion!" Owens yelled.

Sahir Umar had been sitting on the passenger side, seat belt unfastened. He did not believe in them. When his door blew open he flew through the air, scraping his head on the trunk of a tree before hitting the ground, unconscious. His face covered in blood, he appeared to be dead.

The others who had survived the explosion, now in a fight for their life, attempted to find cover and defend themselves from the sudden attack.

What the drivers lacked in marksmanship, they more than made up for in rounds spent, and some of their bullets found their marks. Owens, by far the best shot, picked off a terrorist with just about every shot he took.

The enemy had dwindled down to three or four, the ones who had been able to find the best cover. Most were across the road in the brush behind a rock, the other shielded by the truck. They were highly trained fighters, good with their assault rifles. As they fired, Owens could hear the scream of a driver as he was hit, then a second. This needed to end fast or they would run out of drivers to bring back with them.

"Stay down! I'll try to pick 'em off." He fired another shot.

"Looks like I'm going to have to get behind them," Owens told the others in his small group.

Jabaar cried, "No! You are wounded. I am trained in assault rifles and can run. It was my people who took your friends. This is something I must do."

He grabbed one of the AK-47s they had procured from the cave, and headed through the brush to encircle the last remaining hostiles. It only took him a minute before he could be seen creeping back down the side of the road toward the two remaining shooters hiding there.

Nearing to within fifteen yards Jabaar knelt, took aim and fired. One down. The other one, however, turned quickly, raised slightly to take aim, and returned the fire, hitting Jabaar in the chest. He fell on his back.

The second that the terrorist exposed himself was all Owens needed. He took the bastard down. Only one left, near the damaged truck.

"We've got to get Jabaar off the road!" Owens made a move toward him.

The last remaining hostile took several shots at Owens, pinning him down before he could reach the road. Given the angle, Owens could not return the fire.

Jabaar, though down, was not out. Hearing the shots, he turned onto his stomach, immediately seeing Owens' peril. He crawled closer and took the shot; he did not miss. The last terrorist had been eliminated.

Owens and Jacobs hurried to Jabaar, fearing the worst. They were right; his wound was too severe. He could not be saved.

"No!" Damn it, *no!*" Owens cried.

Jabaar took a couple of shallow breaths, gazed up at his new American friends, then closed his eyes as his head fell back. Not even enough time for Owens to thank him for saving his life.

Both were quiet a few moments; then, Owens said, "We're taking him back with us. I want to tell his family about his bravery. We'll make sure they are proud of their son."

They carried him to the supply truck, putting him down alongside Johnson. "He's a credit to his people," Jacobs said as he covered him with a portion of the tarp.

The drivers had regrouped at the supply truck. "Pick up all the rifles and look for extra ammo," Owens told them. "We don't want to leave anything behind that can be used by others. Then, let's get the hell out of here."

The men hurried to carry out his orders. A minute later Numley called, "Owens, better come over here. One of 'em is still alive, but just barely." He had taken the rifle from the last militant lying next to the overturned truck.

As Owens approached, the terrorist raised his head and glared at him. "You the leader?"

"Yeah, I guess you'd call me that."

"You think you have won, but you haven't...and you won't."

"What do you mean—?"

The man died before he could answer.

℟

For three straight days Commander Buchanan's staff had worked exclusively on locating the missing truckers. They were baffled as to how terrorists and prisoners could disappear for this long. They had contacted all of their intelligence sources to learn of any rumors. The military had many friends in the surrounding area, but none had seen or heard of anything suspicious. It seemed strange that this many people could just disappear without a trace. All the evidence indicated that the missing truck had headed toward Baghdad. But who knew for sure?

The NCIS investigators reported that the only way the terrorists could have transported that many captives would have been in the missing trucks. In fact, one would have been enough, so they questioned why two were taken. They reasoned that if they could find the trucks, they would also find the prisoners and their abductors, or at the very least, discover clues as to where they were being kept.

Commander Buchanan was on the phone with Randall, who had called him again, as he had each day, for any updates. "Just so you know, I'm pulling out all the stops to solve this one. In fact, I was just contemplating my next steps."

"What do you have in mind?"

Randall hoped it wouldn't interfere with his top-secret plan to go out to Camp Mojave after he hung up. He didn't want anything to screw up his delivery of the money, as instructed, to get his men back.

"I want to double check the campsite just to make sure we didn't miss anything. I'm sending my people back out for another look. I tell you this because I want you to know we are doing everything we can under the circumstances."

"When are they going?"

"Later this afternoon. We have some ops to run here first."

"That sounds good. I appreciate it. I will call you if the terrorists contact the television networks again. I've got their promise to call me if contacted. In fact, Fox News said they would delay broadcasting anything new if it would help save the lives of my men."

"Now that's what I call teamwork. Hope I can repay the favor some day."

Hanging up, the Commander buzzed his yeoman, telling him he wanted a chopper to take his best personnel back out to the camp for another look after the ops were completed. "Include a Cobra as escort and direct them to check the terrain along the way."

At this stage he was hoping they might get lucky and spot the missing trucks. Nothing else had worked.

ℜ

By the time the second terrorist truck arrived, the battle was over. Sahir Umar, having feigned death until after the infidels had driven off, stumbled through brush and waved the vehicle down.

"Sahir, what has happened?" his second in command asked.

"We were attacked with a roadside bomb." He was amazed at the ingenuity of the American infidels, but would never admit it. "By the blessing of Allah, I am the only survivor. I saw our supply truck a moment before the explosion. We must leave immediately. We cannot let them get away."

ℜ

After attending to several wounded drivers—Jabaar had been the only fatality—and loading the lead truck with the additional rifles and ammunition, they lumbered along the dirt road for another three hours.

Rounding a bend, there it was: the old campsite where they had lived just one week ago. Or, at least that's where it used to be. Now, only a large pile of rubble stood in its place. The area was deserted. Their hope had been that the military would be there to help, to escort them the rest of the way, but they were still on their own.

The trucks stopped and the canvas tarp raised so the drivers could see what had happened to the camp after they were taken captive. They shook their heads in dismay. All their personal belongings had been destroyed, along with the trucks and buildings.

Still, considering all that each of them had been through, they thought themselves lucky to be alive. Nothing else mattered. Even with all their pain from the wounds and beatings, it could have been worse — a lot worse.

As they prepared to continue on, Jacobs shouted, "Wait a minute!"

Hopping out of the supply truck, he went over to one of the many piles of rubble. He picked something up and brought it back to the truck. It was a remnant of the scarf Lynn had sent him a few weeks earlier. He didn't think he would ever see it again. As they figured the worst was over now that they were not that far from Baghdad, he tied the scarf on the supply truck's antenna. The red, white and blue would fly the rest of the way to celebrate their victory.

"Now, let's get out of here! I'm definitely going to wear that scarf when I see Lynn again. I don't care how hot it is."

They lowered the canvas top and resumed their trek to Baghdad, more relaxed than they had been in over a week, knowing they were almost home.

ℜ

Sahir Umar and his remaining men had caught up to them during the morning hours. Their truck had traveled fast, often taking the many turns on two wheels. This was their domain—that knowledge used to their advantage. They knew no fear and would not be defeated by these men, these infidels.

As they passed the ravaged camp, the dust of the fleeing trucks could be seen ahead. With binoculars, Sahir spotted their missing supply truck. It traveled behind a larger one carrying what looked like a load of crates. He knew better. The lead truck was not full of supplies; it held their prisoners, American infidels who thought they had gotten away from their captors. But it wasn't quite that simple, not when a man like Sahir had sworn vengeance.

They had been caught off guard earlier. But now the element of surprise belonged with Sahir and his men. And these militants were better armed than either of the other two. In addition to an M60 machine gun mounted on the cab of their truck, their arsenal included a shoulder-fired rocket launcher, and the man holding it had the necessary training to use it effectively. As the region was familiar territory, they knew of a shortcut over a small hill that would put the escapees in full view within minutes—and more important, in range of their rocket launcher.

Sahir directed the driver to take the trail just past the campsite that cut across the dry riverbed to a hilltop. "By the time the trucks get there, we will be ready for them."

The rocket launcher would be used to destroy the lead truck and its passengers. The machine gun would take down any survivors, accomplished by driving the truck straight down the hill at them. It would happen fast. There would be no time for them to respond. All would be slaughtered. It had now become more than money—far more.

The M60 machine gun had been stolen from the U.S. Army, which has used this type of general-purpose medium machine gun since the 1950s. It fired 7.62-millimeter ammunition at the rate of 600 shells per minute and could cut a target in half in seconds. With this firepower, Sahir believed the battle would be short lived. At twenty-three pounds, the lightweight weapon was deadly for its size. Placed on a tripod and strategically mounted on the cab of the truck, the man assigned to fire this devastating weapon was provided ample protection from any return fire. Victory was all but assured.

Sahir shouted, "They killed our brethren; they won't live to tell about it. Allah blesses us, not these infidels!"

ℜ

They arrived in plenty of time at a plateau atop the hill alongside the last remaining stretch of dirt road before it connected with a paved highway. Loud singing could be heard from the back of the truck. Sahir smiled for the first time that morning. "They are happy for nothing. That is their last song."

It took only seconds for the rocket launcher to be readied for the attack. Despite the moving target, it would be an easy shot. The infidels were only a couple of hundred yards away, the truck massive. They moved slowly, still on the dirt road.

Sahir conducted the exercise with the skill of a highly trained combatant—which he was. He had not become one of the most feared leaders in the region for nothing. His followers believed he could not be stopped. All were dedicated to him and the cause he represented.

Sahir studied the road below with binoculars and selected a large tree as the target area to fire on the lead truck when it drove past. As the firing instructions were given to the gunner, Sahir spotted a vehicle with a lone driver turn off the highway and head toward the oncoming trucks. At first concerned, he then recalled the original plan. "It must be someone from the trucking company with the ransom." He smiled again.

Although final details had not been confirmed between Sahir and the intermediary before leaving for the cave, he had already been instructed to have the company man come alone to the trucker camp and hide the money there. When the escape had been discovered, all thoughts of the money disappeared. Now he realized that he could have everything—the money and his vengeance.

"Wait until the truck stops for the oncoming car. It will be even easier to hit. Whatever you do, you must not hit the car. Do you understand?"

"Yes *Qa-'id*, I understand."

The rocket launcher, an RPG-7 anti-tank grenade launcher, one of the most common infantry weapons available, is the weapon of choice for many guerrillas around the world. It is relatively cheap, quite effective and found everywhere, as it is manufactured in over forty different countries, including Iran and Iraq. It has a maximum effective range of approximately 325 yards against a moving target and over 500 yards against a stationary one. The truck, at approximately 200 yards away, was well within range. The flight time before impact would be just over one second.

The gunner knelt in the dirt next to the truck, his assistant beside him as they made ready for the attack. It would only be a minute or so. He raised the launcher to his shoulder and aimed it at the truck as he waited for it to spot the oncoming car and stop. The gunner had blown up many automobiles, a tank and even a truck, but not one with so many American infidels on board. The goal would be to hit the truck bed so all would be killed with one shot. His body trembled as he waited for his moment.

The truck with its unsuspecting passengers inched closer toward the oncoming car. The shooter firmed up his finger on the trigger and prayed, " May Allah be with me. This will be my best kill ever—"

He didn't complete his thought. At that moment the shooter and his rocket launcher were flying through the air in pieces, blown apart by a well-aimed missile from a Marine Cobra attack helicopter. The blast killed him, his assistant and many of his brethren in the truck.

Although flying high to minimize the sound of their engines and the two-blade rotors, the pilots of both choppers headed out to Camp Mojave had been carefully examining the terrain as they searched for the missing trucks and a clue to the hidden location of the captured drivers. The ops planned for that day had been cancelled, enabling the choppers to not only leave the base earlier than originally scheduled, but with Commander Buchanan on board.

Having observed the two trucks leaving Camp Mojave, they'd glided silently down to a lower elevation to scrutinize them more closely. Upon seeing the American colors on the smaller truck, their hopes soared. Maybe, by some stroke of luck, these trucks might be carrying the missing men.

They saw the car with its lone driver—a rarity in Iraq— headed toward the trucks. At first they focused solely on it and whether or not it posed a potential danger to the trucks. But then they spotted the men with the rocket launcher on the side of the hill and instantly realized that they were, in fact, the greater danger. Already hovering at the lower elevation, they were in position to take a shot at the terrorists with their own effective weapon, an AGM-65 Maverick air-to-surface missile. They too were good at their job—very good. The shot, a direct hit, blew them to kingdom come, saving the lives of men who had already gone through their own personal version of hell.

After taking out the rocket launcher and the truck, the Cobra, along with the Huey started to strafe the area with their guns—the Cobra with its 20 millimeter turreted cannon and the Huey with its 7.62 millimeter lightweight machine gun—firing at the remaining terrorists as they retreated to the cover of nearby rocks. The Huey's copilot radioed headquarters for additional choppers with troops to search for anyone they might have missed.

Mission accomplished—almost.

ℜ

Sahir, accompanied by two of his men, had squatted beside a large rock to observe the anticipated kill, out of view when the Cobra fired its missile. As he watched the blast destroy the launcher, the truck and most of his men, his plan to avenge Ali's death shattered with it. His life, he knew, was over as well. All was lost. The operation had failed. He didn't know how; it just had. The American infidels would use this failure as propaganda against everyone supporting the cause of Islam. Other progressive Islamic leaders along with their followers would ridicule him and his group, in spite of his many successes. Like it or not, the time had come for him to die as a martyr. Then he would be remembered for his heroism, not his failure.

He informed his men of this dilemma, a problem that impacted them as well, and directed them to follow him down the hill while the American helicopters were busy scattering the others over the hillside. Their goal would be the same as it had been all along: destroy as many infidels as they could before they were sent to Paradise.

"Allah will bless us for this final act of courage."

They began their short descent down the hill, staying low and close to the brush to remain undetected for as long as possible.

ℜ

Jacobs, who had started to film the chopper attack almost immediately after the initial blast, saw Sahir and his men through the telescopic viewfinder. They were armed with rifles. As they ran down the hill toward them, he knew his life and that of the other drivers was still in jeopardy.

Using the walkie-talkie, he alerted Owens about the attack. Owens peered out a small hole in the canvas tarp. "Not to worry. I've got 'em in my sights."

Jacobs slid out the right side of the truck and ducked down beside it for cover when the shooting began. He left the video camera running and pointed in the direction of the attack, realizing this would be a defining moment for them. He didn't want to miss any of it.

Sahir was the first to realize that the drivers no longer sat in the cabs of their trucks. He asked if either of his men had seen them leave. But they had been too preoccupied with their descent to continuously watch the trucks. Sahir directed them to the back of the first truck. "That's where we will find them, cowering in shame."

Jacobs fired the first shot—his last bullet from the Smith & Wesson. It found its mark, hitting Sahir in his right eye. He spiraled to the ground in pain...then total darkness.

"Good luck seeing the seventy-two virgins, asshole," Jacobs muttered.

When the other two saw their leader fall, they began wildly firing their rifles, first in the direction of Jacobs, then at the back of the lead truck, as they had been instructed. Several bullets hit the supply truck, the others passing harmlessly through the canvas top of the lead truck or safely bouncing off its low metal sides.

Owens had stayed hidden long enough. He directed the men to raise the canvas top on the left side, and with a recently acquired and fully loaded AK-47 he systematically dropped the last remaining hostiles in their tracks. It only took two short bursts to cut them in half.

Owens and his men had saved the drivers for the third and final time that day.

ℜ

After the choppers finished sweeping the hillside, they landed on the road between the lone automobile and the two trucks. Embarrassed, the pilots realized they had not completely fulfilled their mission. They saw the bodies of the three terrorists that had carried out what proved to be their last attack on the trucks.

Their embarrassment lasted only a moment. Never had a Marine been better received than the ones in the two choppers. The canvas tarp on the right side flew up;

allowing everyone to see that they had finally reached the safety of their own military. They stood and shouted with joy. Their relief could not be contained. The ones that could, leaped out of the truck and ran or limped toward the choppers. Their injuries almost forgotten, they knew that they had made it—back to civilization and the security it provided.

Commander Buchanan and his pilots were surrounded. Hands were shaken, backs slapped. They found it difficult to believe what they were seeing and feeling, surrounded as they were by the happiest, yet most beat up group of men they had ever encountered

Randall, the bag of money in hand, leaped out of his car to join them. He grinned; he had gotten his men back.

Owens, Jacobs, and Numley remained with the trucks, standing next to the bodies of Johnson and Jabaar. They watched the joy of the other drivers, their arms draped over one another's shoulders. Their self-esteem soared; they knew they had done it. Each had played a critical role in the success of this almost impossible mission. Their rescue plan had worked. They had single-handedly saved these men and returned them to Iraq.

They listened as some of the drivers started to talk at once, attempting to answer the Commander's questions.

"They dropped down into the cave from the back."

"The cave? What cave?"

"Where they kept us. In Iran."

"Iran?

"Yeah."

"By the way, Randall. Your supervisor of the guards was a bad hire. He was their inside guy. He ratted us out. He's tied up in the truck."

Randall looked over at the truck, bewildered.

Commander Buchanan said, "Keep going. Give me details."

"After they came in, the bullets started flying. It was wild."

"Then what happened?"

"We loaded up in trucks, but were followed."

"Followed?"

"Yeah, even more terrorist bastards. We blew them up before reaching Camp Mojave."

The Commander shook his head, "If only we had this on film. I think it's the only way the American public will believe it."

Jacobs smiled. He'd surprise him with the videotape tomorrow. First a dupe had to be made. He thought, *It's the only way my friends will ever believe this either.*

Commander Buchanan then realized he needed the rest of the story. "You keep saying 'they.' Who did all this? Who got to you before we did?"

The drivers looked among themselves, and then back at the trucks. In unison they pointed to the three men still standing next to the supply truck. "They were the ones who got us out, Commander. The old guys...it was the old guys who saved us."

The Commander looked them up and down with the respect one reserves only for the very best. He nodded in admiration, and then did something his men had never seen before. He saluted civilians.

The other Marines quickly took his lead. They snapped to attention and they too saluted these new heroes—the old guys.

Acknowledgements

First and foremost, I want to thank my wife Cherie for her constructive thoughts and toleration of the hours I spent at the computer tinkering with this story during times when we could have gone somewhere...anywhere, and done something...anything, together.

I would also like to thank my editor, Mike Sirota, for his teaching patience with a novice writer, and his invaluable suggestions in revamping and improving this story after I thought I was done. He took my concept and helped me make it a reality.

Lastly, I would like to thank Eric Chauvin for the unique cover design and graphics plus family members, friends, and other sources for their contributions in the form of advice and education on topics that I have little knowledge: Bob Ryan, Google Search Engine, Jason Henry, John Van Doren, Marvin Dove, Book: *What You Need To Know About Islam & Muslims* by George W. Braswell Jr.

Mike Ryan

About The Author

Mike Ryan spent his entire career in the financial community; a stockbroker, founding officer of a life insurance company, and president of a marketing firm. Although Mike has written numerous brochures and magazine articles during his career, *The Old Guys* is his first novel. He currently lives in Southern California with his beloved wife Cherie. They have three children from previous marriages, Julie, Kevin and Laurie. Mike is a graduate of Long Beach State (Sigma Pi Fraternity); and the Naval Officer Candidate School, serving aboard an aircraft carrier in Vietnam. His favorite hobbies are golf, music and reading novels. Like several of his characters, Mike's company forced him out before he wanted to retire. Part of this novel is his story.

Charade

ISBN 142514274-5

9 781425 142742